# THE FIRST BOOK OF **GRABINOULOR**

P. Albert-Birot

THE FIRST BOOK OF **GRABINOULOR**

**EPIC**    BY    **PIERRE ALBERT-BIROT**

TRANSLATED   BY   BARBARA   WRIGHT

IN CONSULTATION WITH ARLETTE ALBERT-BIROT WITH A PREFACE BY

BARBARA WRIGHT AND A POSTFACE BY ARLETTE ALBERT-BIROT

PUBLISHED   BY   ATLAS   PRESS   LONDON   IN   1986

THE DALKEY ARCHIVE PRESS

Parts of this translation have appeared in "Atlas Anthology 3," London,
1985.

ISBN: 0-916583-18-X
Library of Congress Catalog Card Number: 86-072567

Publication partially supported by grants from The National Endowment
for the Arts, a federal agency, and The Illinois Arts Council, a state
agency.

First American Edition

# CONTENTS

# Contents

*WHEN, BY PURE, happy chance, I got to know Pierre Albert-Birot, he was 88, but I never would have guessed it. For the next two and a half years I saw him quite frequently, either in Paris or in the French country-side, and each occasion had a similar kind of magic about it.*

*Part of the magic came from the fact of PAB and his much,* much *younger wife Arlette being the happiest couple I have ever known. And part of it came from PAB's spontaneous communication of his poetic* joie de vivre. *I have vivid memories of him as the animated centre of groups of young poets—or old friends—or new admirers. He was an enthusiastic visitor to art exhibitions and theatres. He was the genial host at Arlette's splendid dinner parties . . .*

*But life hadn't always been like that for Pierre Albert-Birot. His happy childhood was followed by a difficult, poverty-stricken adolescence. His parents' marriage broke up and his mother moved to Paris with her son. There was not enough money for him to continue with his lycée education there but, oddly enough, he was able to study sculpture at the École des Beaux-Arts, because it was free. A first marriage left him, still a very young man, with four children to support, which he did with great difficulty. By the time of the First World War (he was declared unfit for military service) he was beginning to be less interested in all the other arts he had been practising and to want to concentrate on poetry (in its all-embracing sense.) In 1916 he had a sort of revelation. What was needed in those barbarous times, he saw, was an avant-garde review. So he founded one (financing it from his unemployment allowance), and called it 'SIC' (from Sons, Idées, Couleurs, and also from the Latin affirmative adverb.) He had always been a solitary, though, and he knew no one in the world of the arts. So he produced the whole first number of 'SIC' quite alone. By the end of 1919, however, when he decided it had served its purpose, 'SIC' had published all the now-famous names of the period, and Albert-Birot had been responsible for the first staging, in 1917, of Apollinare's* Les Mamelles de Tirésias.

*His second wife, Germaine, was a musician. After she died, and before he met Arlette, he had been for something like a quarter of a century, in his own words, 'excessively, and much too solitary'. Describing his life at the time, he wrote: 'I live two hours a day. I waste twenty-two*

*i*

*in sleeping, doing my domestic chores, and earning enough to live on. These two hours of real life occur after each meal. The whole morning, all I am thinking of is the poetic hour I'm going to have after lunch, and after the meal I feel almost drunk at the thought that in a few moments I shall be immersed in poetry. I go into my work room and it's really, really as if I were walking into heaven.'*

*In these two hours a day PAB produced a vast amount of work. Poems of every conceivable kind: Sound poems, typographical poems, simultaneous poems, poster-poems, square, rectangular, chess-board poems. And even straightforward poems. Plays. Novels. And . . . GRABINOULOR. Grabinoulor sprang, fully armed, from his creator's brain (and heart) in a forest in Royan in 1918. (Arlette Albert-Birot describes his subsequent evolution in her postface.) In 1933 Max Jacob said of Grabinoulor: 'It has been called a masterpiece, as if a work could qualify as such when it's only just been born. A work isn't born a masterpiece, it becomes one. And yet it's saying a lot of a book to call it at the same time: Gay, living, contemporary (I don't like the word modern), intelligent, fantastic, poetic, realistic, daring, more than daring, psychological, synthetic, symbolic, simple, classic, universal, surprising, bizarre, banal, larger than life, true to life and even true to experience, attractive, odious, pessimistic, optimistic, serious, humorous and even more than humorous . . .'*

*Grabinoulor himself—the person—among all his other talents 'can naturally travel at the same time in the past and the future'. Actually, he can do absolutely everything he wants to, yet to my mind he is only slightly more marvellous than his creator. In his manifesto printed in the first number of 'SIC', Pierre Albert-Birot declared:*

> *Our aim is:*
> *To act —*
> *We want:*
> *To look, to see, to hear, to seek, and to*
> *[carry you with us.*
> *To love life, and say so; to live it, and*
> *[invite you to live it with us . . .*

*Don't forget that this aim was professed in 1916. Throughout his life and in all his work, Albert-Birot fulfilled it. Everything about him was positive and joyous—even when life was playing him the dirtiest of dirty tricks.*

> *Listen*
> *say*
> *YES*
> *and you'll make*
> *and you'll make*
> *and you'll make*
> *the sun shine*
> *It's true*
> *Here's my hand on it*
> *YES*

*Albert-Birot was never any good at selling his own work; when the third edition of* Grabinoulor *appeared in 1964, almost none of his previous work was still in print. A lot of it hadn't even been published, and was simply sitting piled up in his wardrobe. Now, however, thanks to Arlette and to the valiant publishers Rougerie, many volumes of his poetry and at least 6 volumes of his plays are available. (And les Editions de l'Allée have just started reissuing his prose works.) In May 1985 I saw his play* Matoum et Tévibar *performed in Paris by a group of young actors. The audience (average age early twenties, I should think) was doubled up with laughter (at all the right places). Albert-Birot's work is indeed timeless.*

*All his plays are in free verse, and all, except* Plutus, *which is a 'free transposition' from Aristophanes, eschew punctuation. For Grabi, PAB knew from the very beginning that he could not possibly use punctuation, having conceived the whole long book (even the then-unwritten parts of it) like the jet of a fountain, in one continuous flow. The reader too soon realizes how impossible punctuation would be.*

*Over the last twenty years, several English publishers have talked vaguely about bringing out a translation of* Grabinoulor, *but this is the first time that one has actually had the courage to do so. The Germans have been more fortunate: Eugen Helmle's translation of* The First Book of Grabinoulor *was published in 1980, and Helmle has also published a translation of the 1919* Poèmes quotidiens, *and a big volume of Albert-Birot's* Poems, 1916-1924. *In Italy,* Barbe-Bleue *and* Matoum et Tévibar *have been performed, and* Matoum *has been published in an annotated* edition (translated and edited by Germana Orlandi.) There has been an anthology in the Slovak language, and there have been theses in various countries . . .

A final word about punctuation. It was in 1917, a whole year before Grabi was even conceived, that PAB declared war (his kind of war) on most forms of it—(although he did still permit himself to use question marks.) His first published book of poems, Trente et un Poèmes de Poche, was printed in April 1917 for Editions 'SIC'. The 31st. of these pocket poems tells us:

> Nature has no full stops
> Day isn't separated from night
> nor life from Death
> enemies are united by their hatred
>
> Væ soli
> Why? Because he doesn't exist
> This book is not
> separated
> from those that will follow it
> and I'm going to stop
> using full stops

—Barbara Wright

# THE FIRST BOOK OF **GRABINOULOR**

# FIRST CHAPTER

*Grabinoulor wakes up*

THAT MORNING Grabinoulor woke up with his heart full of sunshine and his nose standing up straight in the middle of his face a sign of fine weather and just a glance at his friendly blanket showed that it wasn't only his mind that was reaching out to life in virile expectation

While he was happily washing his hairy body he went jumping naked through the woods and published a book then he put his clothes on and even had some compliments from his implacable friend the mirror which isn't in the habit of paying them lightly then he was immense and went into the street where two girls were going by on bicycles so he saw some legs and some undies and he didn't know which girl to choose now while this battle was still raging inside him the objects of his desire had all but disappeared and it infuriated him to see that the road was turning round and going to get them so the part of him that wanted the white dress and the black hair lashed out so decisively that the other part was killed and so thoroughly annihilated that no one has ever been able to find it either in this world or the other

Grabinoulor is much stronger than any cogwheels and especially on the days when his nose is erect as it was that morning for example so then so then he took the girl he'd chosen and went on his way almost immediately he met another girl who was on foot and she was alone Grabinoulor didn't have an opponent so he chose her at first sight and went on more and more happily and even though the shadows of the trees tried to bar his way he passed through Paris where he didn't have any adventures because he was thinking of something else and immediately came back into the Atlantic sub-prefecture he lived in the town of glorious idleness even so while he was walking along the top of a cliff he built a house admirably suited to both winter and summer and painted it yellow and green and for this he needed neither ladders nor pots of paint nor brushes and while he was busy building a machine to transform the movement of the sea into electric light he lay down on the sand and nearly left for Spain but an ant stopped him for Grabinoulor is kind and observant and the ant was finding it very difficult to climb up the mountain which kept trickling down under its feet and that was when he made a hole with his stick to see what the ant would do but he was too strong he dug too deeply and his stick went right through to the other side now as he was very fond of this stick which was itself extremely attached to him he followed it but as the town he came to was in total darkness and fast asleep and he didn't know it he was afraid that he wouldn't be able to find his way around and also perhaps that he might be taken for a murderer so he came straight back up to this side with his stick but the sun had lain down in his place and he didn't want to disturb it so he went off into next year to see whether the war was over and when he got home with a light step he said to his wife are we going to have lunch soon I'm starving


## SECOND CHAPTER

*Grabinoulor tries to find perpendiculars and parallels*

THE STATUETTE was badly made and not perpendicular to its plinth and this caused Grabinoulor some distress because he was always afraid he was going to fall over when he looked at it so he decided to restore its equilibrium and he put a wedge under the plinth and that made the statuette perpendicular to the shelf inside the display cabinet but the plinth was no longer parallel to the shelf and this made Grabinoulor most uneasy so he quickly unwedged the plinth and wedged the shelf then Grabinoulor had a look and felt a bit giddy because the statuette was perpendicular to the base of the display cabinet but the shelf was no longer parallel to the base and Grabinoulor said good god it isn't the shelf that wants wedging it's the cabinet so he did that and then the statuette was exactly perpendicular to the floor of the room but Grabinoulor had to stick out a hand on one side to stop the cabinet falling over which was what it wanted to do and he thought this display cabinet can't exist unless it has its four feet on the ground it's the floor I must raise on one side so he raised the floor and at last the statuette agreed with the plumb-line hanging from Grabinoulor's finger tips but he had to bend one of his legs to keep himself upright and to his great despair he noticed that the floor and all the furniture in the room were no longer parallel to the ceiling so Grabinoulor leaned an elbow on the marble mantlepiece and said out loud I am going to restore the equilibrium and he put the floor back in its place and went out and put a wedge under the house and at last all the lines in the room were parallel to one another but the clocks stopped and the china and glass in the sideboards bedded down together making a great racket and all the tenants in the block began yelling help help the pregnant woman on the third floor went mad on the second floor a man who was having a pee sent it all over the place another on the sixth floor who was about to give his wife a child suddenly found that his centre-bit had gone all soft and there was no more water no more heating no more light some people tried to get down the stairs others started yelling out of the windows and people in the street went to fetch the guardians of the peace who telephoned to the inspector who telephoned to the prefect who telephoned to the minister then they sent the security forces road blocks were set up and the crowd was kept five hundred metres away from both sides of the collapsing house the neighbouring blocks were evacuated and Grabinoulor saw that the floor of the room was parallel to the display cabinet the display cabinet was parallel to the ceiling and all these parallel lines delighted him but he found it difficult to walk or stand upright at this moment he heard a noise in the street and in the house so he went out and immediately the guardians of the peace shouted run for it and it wasn't that he was a coward it was purely by reflex action that he began to run but he soon stopped and thought that he didn't know why they had shouted run for it and he turned round and he was horribly distressed when he saw that his house was no longer but not in the slightest bit perpendicular to the ground and he walked back very slowly his head bowed his hands behind his back because he was thinking very hard and the guardians of public order rushed up to stop him passing but he saw neither the crowd nor the guardians nor the fists trying to get at him so he passed and disappeared and not long afterwards gradually gradually the house regained its peaceful perpendicular and the guardians the fireman the inspectors the ministers fled much more worried than when they arrived and Grabinoulor lit a cigarette

So it wasn't the house that had to be raised on one side but the ground and Grabinoulor immediately decided to go and put a very precisely-calculated wedge under the south part of Paris and he had the satisfaction of seeing that his house was parallel to the ground that the statuette was perfectly vertical and that all the lines in the room were parallel to one another but a lot of houses were collapsing the number of victims was never published fires floods explosions derailments broken bridges the Seine overflowed on to the Right Bank and finally the town was cut off from the rest of the world the engineers were ordered to restore communications and despite great atmospheric interference the Eiffel Tower called for help it recorded radio messages coming in from all over the world apropros of the earthquake that had annihilated a large part of Paris

Grabinoulor was a little worried when he thought of all the crockery he'd broken moreover even though he felt an undeniable satisfaction when he considered that all the houses still standing were indisputably parallel to the ground he felt a no less undeniable embarassment when he observed that all these parallel lines were neither horizontal nor vertical so he worked out the exact amount of his pleasure and his displeasure and discovered that he felt more 'dis' and that made him realize that he hadn't in the least found the equilibrium he'd been looking for and that for the moment it would be better to put Paris back in its place and look for a more perfect more energetic and at the same time more modern solution and he also told himself that it was simpler to let the pundits believe there had been an earthquake because they would have no difficulty in accepting that what one shock had destroyed another shock could restore and he unwedged Paris which immediately went back to its old habits and that was when Grabinoulor had a very clear vision of what had to be done namely quite simply to shift the centre of the Earth and he knew in a flash just how far to the north he had to raise that centre to stop the statuette tilting towards the south and make it decently upright like himself and he closed the two Americas up over each other so that New York more or less fell on top of Montevideo then he took the whole lot and carried it up to the Glacial Arctic Ocean in such a way that Tierra del Fuego went and rubbed shoulders with Lisbon Montevideo was very near Berlin Labrador was nudging Novaya Zemlya and Canada became united with Siberia the great bodies of water followed without Grabinoulor having to bother about them and they formed a new Glacial Ocean off the coast of California and in this way the Earth became fairly and squarely if that's the word elliptical a shape which at all events is now recognized as the best at moving through space so it's not even surprising if the poles became elongated into the shape of a high-explosive shell head although no one has ever been certain about it but the fact remains that several things were changed the Equator passed through Paris and the tropical zone extended from the Cape of Good Hope to the Missouri there were only 50° between each meridian the year had only 320 days and it was even thought that this might present a certain advantage because there were as many men of sixty-five to be seen as we see of fifty as many of ninety as we see of seventy as many of a hundred as we see of eighty but everything became more equal over almost the whole of the Earth the days were equal nearly all year long the whole tropical zone enjoyed a constant temperature which roughly approximated to that of the lovely temperate climate we find every year in June along the south-west coast of France and it was then that the centre became the centre the equator became the favourite place of aviators and poets because things were half as heavy there as they really are but the nearer you got to the poles the heavier they got and in those regions a man found it very difficult to carry even a cork quite a few changes followed in the large or small things of daily life which to the punctilious might seem very much at variance with one of the above lines that talks about greater equality but in any case if all the things reported here didn't exactly happen others did happen which were at least equally extraordinary and in this way or in some other way there were certainly a great many things on the Earth that were new or transformed there were even some in the sky the moon became very small just the size of a coffee cup saucer the ballet of the planets was all out of step neither the eclipses nor the comets arrived at the right time nothing in the sky agreed with the astronomers' calculations any more and they were quite worried for a moment

Grabinoulor admired this new Earth and since nearly all the towns in the world had been annihilated as well as most men he was delighted at the thought of the new towns that were going to be built and the new civilizations that would be created unfortunately though someone had seen him depositing America in the north of Europe and the news spread so that very soon all the men that were left knew that it was Grabinoulor who had changed the shape of the Earth and they got together in a Congress and decided to elect some delegate-chief judges who would con-stitute a high court whose job would be to say whether Grabinoulor should be regarded as a god or a murderer and the delegate-chief judges surprised themselves by not all being of the same opinion some wanted Grabinoulor to be considered the greatest saviour of the human race seeing that he had given this 'race' equality and the temperate zone and the golden mean others wanted him to be chopped up and deformed as he had chopped up and deformed the Earth for they proved that if there was indeed more equality between the days and nights and between the months because of the quasi-suppression of the seasons he was nevertheless guilty of having made a world irremediably doomed to inequality between men since it had of necessity to be under the domination of the aristocracy of the equator and those who were of this opinion were in the majority despite all the efforts of Grabinoulor's partisans who had drawn the attention of the Congress to the fact that the men at the extremities had on the other hand a marked advantage over the men at the equator as they could see a little sliver of the other face of the moon that no one even twisting his neck had ever been able to see and this unquestionably restored the perfect equality so long desired

Grabinoulor was brought in and the result of the vote robbed him of a little of his joy because he felt obliged to conclude from it that his world wasn't perfect and so they gave him the choice between being struck by lightning or restoring the Earth to its vaguely spherical shape so he pulled out his handkerchief to wipe a drip off the tip of his nose and all the delegate-chief judges fled shouting police police every man for himself

Grabinoulor went back to his house in a dream he hadn't yet seen it again because all these innovations had taken his mind off it well it was only with the greatest difficulty that he discovered the statuette in the ruins it was intact and tucked away in a little cave that had somehow been hollowed out for it when everything collapsed and Grabinoulor lost no time in taking it to a house that had just been rebuilt nearby he put it down as it had been at first and the plinth was parallel to the shelf inside the display cabinet but the statuette was still not perpendicular on its plinth so Grabinoulor got furious and he was rather tired too so he put America back where it belonged and went to bed and in any case the worlds are so used to sphericity that with the greatest good-nature and of its own accord the Earth started to become round again

## THIRD CHAPTER

*He has slept well*

EVERY MORNING Grabinoulor was in the habit of honouring his wife and that was why the street belonged to him when he walked so his hands his eyes his lips took her breasts her belly her hips and all her curves and while his head was disappearing between her thighs it occurred to him that it was possible that fishes' tails had an influence on the movement of the waves in the sea so he jumped off the bed with his dibber still in the air and it was just as he was plunging his head into the basin that he began to get to the bottom of the question with all its extraordinary consequences so what probably happened was that the bottom of the question got left at the bottom of the water because when he raised his head he said to his wife did you post the letters then he got lost for a time and found himself back in his adolescence or even in his antenascence and he stayed there for part of that day

In the evening he killed the rich people of France because they didn't like raw fleshly beauty then he composed a poem because he was a poet then he pissed because he was a man

## FOURTH CHAPTER

*Panem et circenses*

GRABINOULOR was turning over and over in his hands all the forms of governments and making pretty geometrical drawings of them but a military band passed by and all the forms followed it Grabinoulor tried to bring them back but he lost them in the crowd and he saw men full of the joys of spring playing at who would come first and the one who came first became a centre of love you could see all the hearts running and jumping with him and when he achieved his object the hearts went back to their places round the arena and clapped their hands and everyone's joy elevated

15

Grabinoulor higher than the best jumper had been elevated by his muscles and desire and as Grabinoulor came down he gave sight to a girl who had beautiful eyes then he went back into last year where we lost sight of him

## FIFTH CHAPTER

### *Four minutes make a month*

ONE DAY Grabinoulor took it into his head to regret all the hours of his life that he hadn't lived and he immediately decided to live every single second but after four minutes he had to stop living that sort of life because he was so tired that he thought he could see death on the horizon and he had already aged by a month but luckily a green and blue dragonfly kindly came and poised in front of him on the tip of a wild oat so while he was watching it he recouped at least two weeks out of the month he'd lost by trying to gain too much and from that point while he was coming and going considering men's love for women some ugly little irritations tried to fall on his neck whereupon Grabinoulor made a face and shook himself all over like a horse exacerbated by flies and the little irritations got scared and retreated telling themselves that they'd come back when they were bigger but an extraordinary thing happened which was that Grabinoulor had completely lost the day the date and the hour of the time he was living in that day and he had gone so far astray that he had practically reached eternity or at the very least its outskirts but when he was beginning with unalloyed pleasure to see things such as he had never seen before some signs got together and came and told him today is Wednesday and within a fifth of a second he had found the date and the hour again and it seemed to him that he was a dog chained up outside its kennel even though he was sitting on the sand by the sea and taking great pleasure in discovering all the shapes of his feet with his hand

SIXTH CHAPTER

*Grabinoulor goes to look for the Empire of the Dead*

IT WAS eleven o'clock on the $n^{th}$ day of his age when Grabinoulor noticed a man riding by on a bicycle and he suddenly thought how amazing it was that that man and that machine would go on living in such elegant equilibrium for as long as they were in movement and he also told himself that all the things that make up the Universe are perpetually moving away from one another and then coming together again and immobility doesn't exist because movement is god so he was satisfied for that day with this certainty which is a convenient sort of thing to take with you on a journey and as in any case just at that moment a young man and a young girl were going by all lit up by love he set off for the Empire of the Dead which he'd heard so much about ever since he was born

Grabinoulor walks admirably on the earth and on the water above and below both in space and in time well now something happened that amazed him most wonderfully everywhere he went life laughed in his face and this delighted Grabinoulor because as he'd always heard people talking so crossly about that hegemonic empire he was a bit apprehensive about setting foot or eyes on it even though just the thought of seeing his mother again made him feel happy and he quite looked forward to seeing some famous men and not just having a charming Urbis Romæ-type conversation but there was so much light everywhere that he gradually forgot why he had started out and he went on just for the pleasure of going on

On his way he had occasion to meet a queen enjoying herself in the arms of a cowherd and a marchioness admiring the mouth and dibber of one of the luxury hotel negroes as well as his way of using them and as Grabinoulor was telling this without mentioning names and without comment to the wife of a fellow who worked in a ministry who happened to be giving him tea she protested violently and said that in her opinion the queen and the marchioness were shameless hussies and she told Grabinoulor straight out that she would never compromise herself in such a way but that if she did happen to deceive her husband it would never be with a doorman or with a colleague or with the deputy chief clerk but at

17

the very least with his head clerk and it was very soon  afterwards that
Grabinoulor happened absolutely by chance to see a king and a shep-
herdess coupling and Grabinoulor kept going because he's never tired

In spite of the light that surrounded him as he walked even when it
seemed to be night time he remembered because after all he wants what he
wants that he had started out to go and see the Empire of the Dead and he
had never met as many lovers as he did that day which after all doesn't
prove a thing and he kept asking passers-by could you tell me the way to
the Dead please but some of them took to their heels and didn't look back
others made as if to call a guardian of the peace and a lot of them gave him
hell and threatened to break a stick or an umbrella on his occiput so
Grabinoulor decided that people are really very unhelpful but just then he
remembered that other people before him had made the same journey and
he immediately read through the guidebooks from Homer to Lucian to
Virgil to Dante and even several less well-known but very well-documented
mortographers and he found some very valuable information about this
famous Empire in them with some very beautiful descriptions of the landscapes mountains valleys waterways colours smells means of locomotion
habits customs games and occupations of the Dead with their most recent
opinion of the living and the way to get there and the precautions to take
before entering the Empire and how to behave in it so Grabinoulor got
ready to follow scrupulously all the guide-lines laid down by these
conscientious authors whose world reputation offers all the guarantees you
could possibly desire but there was still one thing that worried him a bit
and embarassed him for a moment and this was the fact that there were
appreciable differences between them as to the precise place where this
Empire is situated but a minute later Grabinoulor thought that naturally
an empire has colonies so he immediately decided to follow all his guides
successively or perhaps simultaneously he's perfectly capable of it and he
so enjoys speed in order to acquire a thorough knowledge of the Empire in
the twinkling of an eye and he went on again and this time he refused to
be distracted by anything on the way whether the tennis players those
healthy-faced wills-of-iron always trying to oppose the desires of the balls
or the marriage of a puppet Romeo and Juliet or the impossibility of anything other than possible things happening or it being time to eat or time
to dibble or time to sleep Grabinoulor went on and on

Now here's something that may seem incredible neither on the
Earth nor in the Heavens did he find what the guides described and yet he

studied them all one after the other and went everywhere they sent him and even to all the other places which in any case were hardly even places any more and he had no alternative but to admit that these explorers of far-off countries had been rather making fools of people by thus declaring that all the dead were cooped up in one small spot and Grabinoulor was knocked sideways by the thought that so many men over such a long time had been able to believe in death and had been pleased to drive themselves to despair by imagining a dead world opposite the living world as if such a thing were really possible and Grabinoulor saw very clearly that his mother was the rose blooming beside him and the forest he was walking through and the birds flying the children playing the lovers passing by the light illuminating them and then he was filled with joy and he admired the world and when he was back home it was with great satisfaction that he watched his old neighbour over the road bending down over the earth and watering caressing caring for and lovingly contemplating his tomatoes his carrots his turnips his onions his lettuces and just at that moment the old man bent down even lower and when he had straightened up again he called his daughter and standing there with his hands dangling and with fury in his voice he said a fat worm ate two of my cos lettuces today but I've just found it under the stalk of the second one and killed it

## SEVENTH CHAPTER

*Grabinoulor the pagan builds the Tower of Life*

WHILE GRABINOULOR was under an oak tree an acorn fell on his head* and he thought about several things first of all that acorn was glans in Latin and that he too had a glans and as a result he was a sort of cousin of the oak tree next that if a man is an acorn he can't be a pig and that as a result we are labouring under a total misapprehension when we give him that name a misapprehension that can be neither agreeeable nor profitable either to man or pig and next that there are only two sorts of line—what a misfortune for people like us and it seems impossible to hope for the slightest improvement—the curve that belongs let's say to God and the straight line that belongs to man which already says a great deal about the quality of his spirit but man often borrows from God though God never borrows from man and just at that moment Grabinoulor going flat out along a curve that was maybe divine maybe human but without the slightest doubt incomparably more audacious than all those created by our engineers was transported behind the war where he saw jackets marching with an empty sleeve swinging and useless trouser legs pinned up at the top of the thigh because an army is a marching forest from which war lops a great many branches and a great many roots but as war still hasn't lopped everything the army is still a marching forest that grows green again and Grabinoulor decided that the Earth is a lovely dance hall and he heard songs coming from the Past and songs coming from the Future so he made his way over towards the songs because Grabinoulor naturally moves at the same time in the Past and the Future although he doesn't do the splits between them because he claims they're the same thing

Grabinoulor was a little surprised because he could neither see the people who were singing nor the place where they might be and their songs mingled with the hymns of the Catholics the psalms of the Protestants the verses of the Jews the whistling of locomotives the klaxoning of motor cars the street cries of traders the shooting of pacifists the lyricism of merry market women the rattle of horse-drawn vehicles the barking of dogs the orchestras of dance halls the desires of the poor the yawns of the rich the laughs of imbeciles and these in particular made a very loud noise which was sometimes louder than all the rest put together and while Grabinoulor was trying to insulate the invisible songs and singers he stepped over a jour de fête that's to say a jour de bêtes without even noticing and the songs soon became familiar to him they celebrated the male with his beautiful dibber and the female with her black triangle and Grabinoulor was as happy as a man who gets up very early in the morning one French June day and while he was listening to these ejaculating poems by means of an insulator of his own invention simply controlled by his willpower he recorded them on a gramophone disc as big as a railway turntable then he built a tower a third of which was made of pink marble sheathed in polished steel and the rest was made of crystal and he put the gramophone in the Tower of Life and the tower revolved keeping perfect time with the Earth so that the orifice of the loudspeaker was always facing the sun and this is how the things in the interior of the tower were and what things were to be found in it

In the centre like a naval gun aimed for long-range firing there rose up a gigantic phallus made of natural bronze polished like a mirror and ablaze with every kind of light its vertex practically touching the cupola and this may well have looked like a bizarre observatory but it wasn't one and as for the base of this strange telescope clamped on its two nicely-distended testicles it looked as if it was emerging from the earth and engraved on the steel sheathing encompassing it were phalluses with wings like birds black triangles breasts bellies animated geometrical figures all of which were singing and every song and poem on the gramophone was also written in the steel and the Tower was much bigger than all the prayerful Saint Peters and on the day of the fête of the sexes all the humans on Earth sang and recited in unison with the gramophone and here are some of the things that were engraved

---

The French version of the following chapter is given, for while it is possible to do justice to some of the poems, it is impossible to do justice to others ('Sains / Seins / O coussins / O mes Saints', for instance, and 'Peau à peau / Sans chapeaux / Ni drapeau / Qu'ils sont beaux / Peau à peau'.) In such cases we have chosen to give a simple literal version of their meaning. (Translator's note)

## HUITIÉME CHAPITRE

*Poèmes à la Chair*

LE POÈTE dira au compas la joie des courbes de l'amour qui sont des lumières que l'on touche et les deux portes sont fermées et il y a de l' ombre sur les pieds et sur les têtes

Mais les désirs vont en ligne droite et pourtant le fauteuil insipide reste toujours dans la même attitude la glace imbécile prend inlassablement le mâle et la femelle mais ne se souviendra de rien

Et eux non plus n'ont pas de souvenirs parce qu'ils dévorent le présent qui marche sur leurs quatre jambes et flambe entre leurs mains

La cheminée est en marbre blanc les mains sont carnivores les bouts des seins sont roses et les mains sont des yeux qui ne mentent jamais les mains sont des yeux des dieux vivants au service des hommes

Le mâle arc-bouté supporte la femelle arquée et la mâle prend et la femelle donne et la lampe est sur la table comme un soleil apprivoisé

Et cependant le mâle et la femelle s'évadent sur le poème à deux voix que chante la main de l'homme

*

## EIGHTH CHAPTER

*Poems to the Flesh*

THE POET will speak to the compass and tell it of the joy of love's curves which are lights that you can touch and both doors are closed and there's light on their feet and on their hands

But desires travel in a straight line and yet the insipid armchair remains in the same attitude the imbecilic mirror tirelessly captures the male and the female but it won't remember anything

And they have no memories either because they are devouring the present which is walking on their four legs and blazing between their hands

The fireplace is made of white marble their hands are carnivores the tips of her breasts are pink and their hands are eyes that never lie for their hands are the eyes of living gods who are in the service of men

The buttressed male supports the arched female and the male takes and the female gives and the lamp is on the table like a tamed sun

And meanwhile the male and the female escape on the poem in two voices which the man's hand is singing

Mon oiseau veut ton nid
　　Marie

　　　　　*

　　Prends garde Lucas
　　Mon chat
　　Mangera ton oiseau

　　　　　*

　　　　Jeanne ma bien-aimée
　　　Bâton d'amour est baguette de fée

　　　　　*

　　　　Le Yoni de ma Rose
　　　　A bagué mon linga

　　　　　*

BOUCHE QUI PREND SI BIEN LA FORME DE LA BOUCHE
INTÉRIEUR FLEUR DE CHAIR QUI VEUT LA CHAIR
DE L'ÊTRE OUBLIÉ DEHORS PAR LE CRÉATEUR

24

My bird wants to nest in your tree
Marie

\*

Take care Lucas
My puss
Will eat yor bird

\*

Jeanne my beloved
Love's sceptre is a magic wand

\*

My Rose's yoni
Has ringed my lingam

\*

MOUTH THAT SO BEAUTIFULLY ASSUMES THE SHAPE OF THE MOUTH
FLOWER OF FLESH THAT SEEKS THE FLESH
INTERIOR OF THE BEING LEFT OUTSIDE BY THE CREATOR

**25**

*

Je voudrais que nous soyons unis
Comme croûte et mie

*

Viens demain
Mettre ton bijou dans mon écrin

*

Un gros Bonheur-des-Dames
Demande un petit bonheur-des-Hommes

*

Jeannette aimons-nous veux-tu
Je mettrai
Une queue à ta rose

*

*

I want us to become one
Like crust and crumb

*

Come tomorrow
And put your jewel in my jewel case

*

A big Joy-of-Women
Wants a snug Joy-of-Men

*

Jeannette come be my love
I will give your rose
A tail

*

LE POÈTE SALUE LE DIVIN
ÉJACULATEUR AU GESTE MA
GNIFIQUE SCEPTRE BIEN EN
MAIN QUE TU ES BEAU DANS
TA DRESSÉE SUPERBE SO
LEIL DE VOULOIR AMOURE
UX DE ZÉNITH QUE TU ES
BEAU DANS TA FORME ARQ
UÉE ET BRAQUÉE VER L'A
VENIR QUE TU ES BEAU DA
NS TA MATIÈRE POLIE ET DU
RE TU ES PLUS BEAU QUE CE
QUE TU ADMIRES TU ES PLUS
BEAU QUE TOUT CE QUI EST
BEAU DIEU VISIBLE DONNÉ
PAR DIEU A CHAQUE HOMME
LE POÈTE VEUT TE REBÂTIR
UN TEMPLE LUMINEUX EN
GUIRLANDÉ DE POÉSIE OÙ
L'ON POURRA VENIR ADMI
RER TON IMAGE D'OR AUSSI
HAUTE QUE LE TEMPLE
ET TE FÊTER TOI QUE DE
PUIS DEUX MILLE ANS NO
US AVONS RENIÉ TOI LE CE
NTRAL TOI L'AFFIRMATIF

# VENITE ADOREMUS

TOUT DISPARAÎT QUAND PARAÎT LE TRIANGLE N
OIR LE TRIANGLE LYRIQUE LE TRIANGLE CEN
TRAL CHANTE ÉPERDUMENT LA DRESSÉE D
U MAÎTRE ET LE TRIANGLE NOIR AVEUG
LE LE DÉSIR QUI LE REGARDE LE DÉSI
R CENTRIPÈTE AUX MAINS SOUPLES
MAIS LE TRIANGLE NOIR EST UN D
ÉSIR SANS MAINS ET LE MÂLE
ASSERVIT CE DIEU FRISÉ ET
LE TRIANGLE NOIR EST D
ANS LA MAIN DE L'HOM
ME ET C'EST A CHAQ
UE INSTANT LA F
IN D'UN MOND
E EXPLOSAN
T DANS LE
S ESPA
C E S

THE POET SALUTES THE DIVINE
EJACULATOR WITH THE MAGN
IFICENT ACTION SCEPTRE WELL
IN HAND HOW BEAUTIFUL YOU
ARE IN YOUR PROUD UPTHRUST
SUN OF THE WILL LOVER OF TH
E ZENITH HOW BEAUTIFUL YOU
ARE IN YOUR CAMBERED SHAPE
DIRECTED TOWARDS THE FUTU
RE HOW BEAUTIFUL YOU ARE I
N YOUR HARD BURNISHED SUB
STANCE YOU ARE MORE BEAUT
IFUL THAN WHAT YOU ADMIRE
YOU ARE MORE BEAUTIFUL TH
AN EVERYTHING THAT IS BEA
UTIFUL A VISIBLE GOD GIVEN B
Y GOD TO EVERY MAN THE POE
T WANTS TO BUILD YOU A NEW
LUMINOUS TEMPLE GARLANDE
D WITH POETRY WHERE PEOP
LE WILL BE ABLE TO ADMIRE
YOUR GOLDEN IMAGE OF TH
E SAME TOWERING HEIGHT AS
THE  TEMPLE  AND  CELEBRA
TE YOU YOU WHO FOR TWO TH
OUSAND YEARS HAD REPUDIAT
ED US YOU THE CENTRAL P
OINT YOU THE AFFIRMATIVE

# VENITE ADOREMUS

EVERYTHING DISAPPEARS WHEN THE BLACK TRIAN
GLE APPEARS THE LYRICAL TRIANGLE THE CEN
TRAL TRIANGLE SINGS ECSTATICALLY OF THE
E UPTHRUST OF THE MASTER AND THE BLA
CK TRIANGLE BLINDS THE DESIRE THAT
GAZES AT IT THE CENTRIPETAL DESI
RE WITH THE LITHE HANDS BUT TH
E BLACK TRIANGLE IS A DESIRE
THAT HAS NO HANDS AND THE
MALE SUBDUES THIS CURLY
GOD AND THE BLACK TRI
ANGLE IS IN THE MAN
'S HAND AND EVERY
INSTANT IS THE
END OF A WOR
LD EXPLODI
NG INTO
INFIN
ITY

*

Corps et corps
Vous vous rappelez les temps où vous n'étiez qu'un corps
Le corps va au corps
La chair à la chair
Le souvenir
Veut tant vous réunir
Saillie au creux
Corps moitié du monde
Qui cherche l'autre Monde
Dont le poète dévot voudrait faire le tour
O mâle ô femelle
Aimez votre beauté

*

Peau à peau
Sans chapeau
Ni drapeaux
Qu'ils sont beaux
Peau à peau

*

*

Body and body
You remember the days when you were only a body
The body moves towards the body
The flesh to the flesh
Remembrance
Wants so much to enmesh you
Salience in hollow
Body half the world
That seeks the other World
Which the devout poet wants to engirdle
O male O female
Love your own beauty

*

Skin to skin
With neither hat
Nor flags
How beautiful they are
Skin to skin

*

Seins seins riches seins printaniers
Rudes seins de femme
Portmanteaux à deux têtes
Qui allez toujours tout seuls devant
Les hommes ont eu l'idée du droit en vous regardent
Mais les hommes saints
Ont dit cachez ce sein
O seins
Précurseurs
Droituriers
Nous vous rendons la liberté
Nous qui vous regardons en face
O seins pleins d'honnêteté

*

Sains
Seins
O coussins
O mes saints

*

Breasts breasts full vernal breasts
Woman's earthy breasts
Portmanteau with two heads
Which always lead the way on their own
Men got the idea of the straight line by looking at you
But saintly men
Said hide that breast*
O breasts
Straightforward
Precursors
Those of us who look straight at you
We give you back your liberty
O breasts full of honesty


*


Healthy
Breasts
O cushions
O my saints


*

O VOUS LES SEINS PLENITUDE DES MAINS REPRESENT- ANTS DE LA COURBE SUR LA TERRE ENCORBELLEMENTS

O VOUS LES SEINS AUDACIEUX QUI N'AVEZ PAS PEUR DU VIDE PROVOCATEURS DE L'AMOUR EVOCATEURS DE LA CERTITUDE

O YOU BREASTS PLENTUDE FOR THE HANDS REPRESEN- TATIVES OF THE TERRESTRIAL CURVE ENCORBELLMENTS

O YOU BREASTS BRAVELY UNAFRAID OF THE VOID ■ PROVOCATIVE OF LOVE EVOCATIVE OF CERTAINTY

*

Le poète a posé sa main sur sa tête et il sent son poème
Comme le père sent l'enfant dans le ventre de la mère
Demain matin les arbres seront verts
La chair
Fait une aube dans la chambre
Tous les objets font silence
Le mâle est en adoration
Et tend ses lèvres vers l'aurore
C'est ainsi

*

C'est une proie que l'on écrase et qui vous éblouit
Nos corps sont des soleils enfermés dans des lanternes sourdes
La robe fut arrachée d'un seul coup
Le ventre s'aplatit sur le ventre éclairent
Et tout le paysage
S'est refermé sur eux

*

Le Mâle a labouré
Le ventre est un dôme
Ave Maria

*

O

TOI LE GOURMAND DE LUMIÈRE VENTRE IMAGE DE LA PERFECTION OFFERTE AUX YEUX ET AUX MAINS

*

The poet has placed his hand on his head and he feels his poem
As the father feels the child in the belly of the mother
Tomorrow morning the trees will be green
The flesh
Brings the break of day into the room
All the objects fall silent
The male is worshipping
And extends his lips to the dawn
It is thus

*

It's a prey which you crush and which dazzles you
Our bodies are suns absorbed within dark lanterns
The dress was torn off
The belly flattens itself on the illuminant belly
And the entire landscape
Is absorbed within them

*

The Male has ploughed
The belly is a dome
Ave Maria

*

O

YOU WHO ARE GREEDY FOR LIGHT BELLY IMAGE OF PERFECTION OFFERED TO THE EYES AND TO THE HANDS

Le matin quand le mâle ouvre les yeux son regard vient s'arrondir
sur les seins de la femelle endormie la vie est blonde blanche et rose et la
force du mâle se dresse au bas de son beau ventre
Le soleil idéalise les rideaux

*

Le poète est un prêtre architecte sculpteur et musicien
Il construira dans l'espace et dans le temps
Un monument grand comme une admiration
Au couple humain

*

Quand la chair apparaît c'est comme un chant qu'on pourrait toucher
Comment comment de si beaux chants peuvent-ils si longtemps si long-
temps
Être étouffés sous les robes qu'importe la couleur des choses et l'heure
Voici l'hymne à la déesse avec ses blancs ses blondes ses roses et ses noirs
Et ses courbes les lèvres savent prendre la forme de toutes ces courbes
Et les lèvres se souviennent comme les mains et voici l'illumination
La fête est éblouissante l'encrier a l'air d'être sur la table
Oh oh oh hi hi hi hi hi hi krrrrrrr krrrrrrrrr A A A A Ha
La chambre penche d'un côté il y a des petits cris dans tous les coins
Bouche bouche touche couche souche la joie sort par la bouche
La chair de l'un est plus blanche que la chair de l'autre mais leurs désirs
ont le même poids la femelle centripétiste tourne autour du mâle
Comme la terre autour du soleil drame cosmique de tous les jours
Deux mondes se sont rencontrés et c'est un nouveau monde
La femme a disparu dans les bras de l'homme le lit est un autel
Et le ciel sera beau quand l'homme marchera au milieu de la route

In the morning when the male opens his eyes his gaze expands to
encompass the breasts of the sleeping female life is blonde white and pink
and the male's vigour rises in the lower part of his beautiful belly
The sun idealizes the curtains

\*

The poet is a priest architect sculptor and musician
He will build both in space and in time
A monument as great as an act of worship
To the human couple

\*

When the flesh appears it's like a song that you could touch
How can such beautiful songs for so long for so long
Be smothered under dresses what do the colour of things and the time
matter
This is the hymn to the goddess with her whites her blondes her pinks and
her blacks
And her curves lips can assume the shape of all those curves
And lips remember like hands and the illumination has appeared
The celebration is glorious the ink-well looks as if it's on the table
Oh oh oh hi hi hi hi hi hi krrrrrrr krrrrrrrrr A A A A Ha
The bedroom is tilting to one side and there are little cries in all the
corners
Mouth mouth touch couch roots joy comes out through the mouth
The flesh of the one is whiter than the flesh of the other but their desires
are of the same weight the centripetal female revolves round the male
As the earth round the sun the everyday cosmic drama
Two worlds have met and created a new world
The woman has disappeared in the arms of the man the bed is an altar
And the heavens will be beautiful when man at last walks in the middle of
the road

## NINTH CHAPTER

*Grabinoulor goes into reverse gear*

GRABINOULOR LOST HIMSELF for a moment in the heavens so as to find his way on Earth again for he could neither detach himself from the two stonecutters he had just seen sawing their section under the orders of the admirable set-square nor from the naked woman he'd seen the day before who was still holding him by his central kingpin nor from a shoe that was hurting his foot so he turned his back and returned to a time that no longer exists which only two-thirds did him good because he was instantly separated from the stonecutters and even from the shoe that hurt him but the naked woman became even more luminous and hotter and the famous kingpin became so threatening that it was touch and go whether they wouldn't once again be as it were pinned to each other but at this time Grabinoulor wanted a different sort of joy so he grabbed hold of Grabinoulor by his two shoulders and they jostled each other along for a step after which he found himself alone in his day-before-yesterday but there was a drifting fog and while he could just see the vague shapes of people calling their bitch by the name of a Roman goddess* he couldn't see the bitch so he receded a bit farther and as he receded the fog thinned so he stopped for a moment in the preceding month because he had quite a clear view of a splendid fireworks display with rockets shooting up in swooning curves and fanning out against the dark sky in descending blue green or gold sheafs which made the whole of the assembled population go Ah then when he got back to the moment before the fireworks had begun he couldn't see anything any more so he passed by and went leisurely back to more than a year before and there the visibility was something like it is in the yellowish dawn of a winter's day and yet it was four o'clock in the afternoon one first day of spring in Paris then the red metallic firemen enchanted the streets by sounding the All-clear and in spite of everything a bright sun was visible and it brought all the people to their windows their doorsteps the pavements the roads then they heard talk of men chopped up of women with their heads cut off then one then some then all of them came up from the cellars then they all went down again and Grabinoulor saw Grabinoulor go down too and he was furious because he was not a subterranean man then the firemen went by in the streets with their sirens that were terribly frightened and their harsh bugles that were bawling at people to be on their guard then the firemen came out of their fire stations then at regualr intervals you could hear explosions that somewhat upset the habits of your heart and mind then Grabinoulor took an extra-big stride to step across all the rest of the Great War and his foot alighted in a time when tobacco was to be found in tobacco shops and he told himself that this was the moment to get in a stock because it would be in short supply all through the war and for a good long time after but as it so happened he found Grabinoulor actually in the process of buying a packet and he had no reason to want to buy any more no point in insisting so Grabinoulor passed by and walked a few steps with his eyes closed and when he opened them again he found that he could no longer recognize anything around him and to start with the light was as mysterious as it is on a day when there's a solar eclipse the objects had shadows that didn't resemble them and after that it was more like artificial lighting everything had its own differently-coloured light and everything appeared and disappeared capriciously which gave the appearance of great disorder such as you find in a World Fair the day before it opens and there was an Assyrian king offering up a sacrifice there was a Gothic cathedral with a coronation a fête in a town in Atlantis the first flight of the Montgolfier brothers Heloise in Abelard's arms the Grands Boulevards in Paris after the 1870 war the poetess Chou Shou-Ch'en chatting with Victor Hugo and they were all laughing singing shouting speaking but whether they were each speaking their maternal language or all speaking the lost natural and universal language we can't be sure and this is a pity but Grabinoulor heard that they weren't making any noise no sound vibrated in the air which was perhaps not air and for a moment Grabinoulor believed himself to be an idea but in the midst of all the agitation that he couldn't hear he soon realized that he had gone back a bit too far before the time of his birth so after some thought he chose to come back to the hour on his watch and on his way back he met himself as an adolescent it was charming but he saw that he was so stupid that with a single leap he found himself back in front of the roast beef which was  beginning to get bored with waiting and it was even possible that the beef was on the point of turning back into veal

## TENTH CHAPTER

*He declares that the portraits of Father Time are poor likenesses*

NAKED AND WET ALL OVER with sea water Grabinoulor climbed right up to the top of a very very high dune to offer if we can call it that his body to the sun and to stretch out on the warm sand and while he was lying there with the whole length of his legs and arms parallel to the slope of the dune he felt for a moment a desire to be no more than an approximately cylindrical body at the top of a very steep slope and he began to roll and he willed himself to obey the law to the very end and he gathered such momentum that he got as far as Eternity and it was there that he had an opportunity to see Father Time in the garage and to be greatly astonished for he had always been told that Father Time was an old man with a big fluttering beard heavy wings and a sickle what's more all the portraits of him represent him like this so he noted that it was pure invention and that once again men had made a mistake because Father Time was quite simply a patient and well-regulated tank and he was amazed then that this tank had passed over the world so often and still not pulverized it which proves beyond a doubt how extraordinarily supple and extraordinarily resistant the world is and Grabinoulor suddenly realized that the tank had just passed over him it's true he had hardly felt a thing but having thought it over he was frightened when he saw the tank coming back at him without hesitation he ran over to another side and while he was running with no other idea than the idea of running the road was suddenly blocked by a dark crowd of motionless and relatively voiceless people who kept repeating very quietly it's awful it's awful and the sun could no longer get through nor could Grabinoulor and he remembered these lines[*]

There may well be some sorrows in store for the days to come
Never mind we all have them
And I certainly have some in the attic of my soul
But we don't live in the attic

and as he couldn't make any headway he told himself that here was a chance to go up into that attic where he immediately arrived and what a lot of old forgotten stuff he found in all its nooks and crannies heaps of shrivelled-up little sorrows what a picture and Grabinoulor stuck his head out of the skylight and looked up into the air

## ELEVENTH CHAPTER

### Admiration

I stood in front of the houses in the town
And I said How admirable
I stood in front of the wheels and the machines
And I said How admirable
I stood in front of the immobile mountains
And I said How admirable
I stood in front of the blue seas and the green seas
And I said How admiarble
I stood in front of the trees in the forests
And I said How admirable
And I stood in front of the big animals
And I said How admirable
And I stood in front of the small animals
And I said How admirable
And I stood in front of women
And I said How admirable
And I stood in front of men
And I said How admirable
I stood in front of the shade
And I said How admirable
And in front of the light
And I said how admirable
Because I looked

Grabinoulor with his eyes shut or perhaps after all open saw this poem inscribing itself at its zenith but without letters of course and when he had finished immobilizing it on paper with the aid of writing he thought that philosophers are very boring and he began to laugh even though he often took the greatest pleasure in listening to them and then as he remembered that he had one day looked everywhere for Death and not found it he told himself that there was still one place he had forgotten viz books by philosophers and he went and sat down on the highest leaf of the sunlit tree in front of him whence he saw very distinctly that there are people who move into the shade and others into the sunlight and therefore war is on earth just as life is and at the very moment of this more or less resounding conclusion what should he see going by beneath him but a teacher of grammar flogging a young poet and Grabinoulor shuddered so hard that he fell down on to the teacher who was squashed flat like an opera hat so Grabinoulor threw a pinch of earth over him to make him disappear and then he invited little Matoum* to lunch

## TWELFTH CHAPTER

### What is the Beyond

THAT DAY Grabinoulor felt cold so he folded away all his inquiring looks and resumed the ordinary size of a town-dweller and this made it possible for him to go into the house and there he saw what had happened

The house no longer had the same sound because the woman who gets called Madame no longer had the same appearance and whereas the one who formerly presided over the table had weighed them all down with her substantial majesty and from her heights had often said in honeyed tones little Angèle doesn't feel the draughts by the time Grabinoulor returned Her Majesty had taken a tumble and little Angèle was on the throne Be very careful with my china she said to the parlourmaid/ major-domo and then resumed her interrupted conversation I repeated my phrase several times but that gentleman didn't seem to understand me I talk perfectly proper though I hope Marie you will order my limousine for two o'clock and Grabinoulor enjoyed himself a lot all through this dinner which didn't seem too long to him because in any case while he was Grabinouloresquely putting away a rather fine series of culinary successes he suddenly remembered the definition of the skimming ladle namely

50

holes surrounded by some iron but the next day all this had become the same colour as everything else and Grabinoulor could see nothing but the walls which hadn't anything to say to him whereupon as he was beginning to feel bored he elegantly passed through those stupid walls and ran over towards the horizon but unfortunately whether because the cold took his breath away or because his legs were less agile he never managed to reach vanishing point that morning in spite of the mountains he strode over the forests he crossed and more or less apropos of this he remembered that one sun-blessed day he had seen a beautiful child playing the trumpet by blowing down the end of a stick and Grabinoulor may well have been a little jealous of this poet however as he was hungry and it was midday he quite simply went to the meatmonger to buy a steak and that morning he found the butcher who was as weighty as a prize pig carefully preparing a steak for a customer his neighbour the wife of the coal-merchant-cum-café-owner and Grabinoulor had to wait ages to be served because the butcher kept interrupting his knife's work and saying to the coal-merchant's wife there's nothing I can do about it Madame Dioudona I simply can't understand what the Beyond is I know some say there's something there but no one has ever come back to say either what it's made of or where it is Ah the Beyond what a mystery I think about it very often Madame Dioudona and the steak Grabinoulor ate that day was really first class and the butcher had given him good weight

## THIRTEENTH CHAPTER

### *Ideas of Paradise*

GRABINOULOR HAD BEEN LIVING in a room for some days and he thought he was dead that's to say he would have been quite prepared to receive a visit from the cellaress of the Kingdom of Satan* if he hadn't just in time remembered his discovery one warm morning of the Immortality-Omnibus and the extraordinary journey he had undertaken that morning to find Death though he hadn't been able to meet it anywhere so he concluded that neither was it in the room he had been living in for several days and that he was well and truly alive even though he didn't seem to be and it was at this point that he tried not as was his wont to pass through its walls but simply to look through them and for a long time all he could see was the wall which greatly astonished and even slightly worried him for this had never happened to him before so he stayed cooped up there and paced up and down within himself and he discovered with pleasure that for his especial benefit the room contained all sorts of sunlit landscapes full of people and colours walking around for no other purpose than to entertain him and without thinking he himself began to walk along the seashore where he caught the sound and stole a look at the shapes of the girls laughing and bathing and the extraordinary thing was that after this larceny the girls didn't seem to have changed in any way some didn't even realize Grabinoulor had stolen anything from them and for his part the more shapes and laughs he purloined the lighter he felt so where did he put all those breasts all those bellies all those laughs what does it matter with Grabinoulor questions of that nature are quite inappropriate so be it and Grabinoulor too soon went into the sea and as he did every time he bathed he felt the pure joy of living through Genesis and when he came out and after running a hundred metres had thrown himself down on the amiable sand he was Adam whom God had just animated so he sometimes half-opened his eyes to let the light in and then shut them again to keep it there and sometimes a voice very close to him asked him something he looked and it was Eve stretching her limbs by his side Eve whose white flesh was visible under a bathing costume whose black silk was so fine that the hollow of her navel looked like a black dot on the semi-transparent ensemble and the tips of her breasts were two very wilful pink dots and Grabinoulor looked at the sky looked at Eve closed his eyes and his chest expanded and his muscles tried to find their own weight and space and he felt himself growing bigger becoming immense as infinite as the light that had engendered him and it was at this moment that he emerged from himself because he realized that his lingam had become a bludgeon

## FOURTEENTH CHAPTER

*Grabinoulor is an elector*

STOP THIEF STOP THIEF people were yelling with all their might at the fugitive while the firemen were directing a mighty jet of water at a fire—which even so is much easier because the fire stays put whereas the thief runs away—their yells penetrated many ears and many windows and many doors opened and at the same time many legs started running along the pavement and every hand tried to get a violent hold on the person who had stolen something from someone and Grabinoulor got carried away by these yells which kept catapulting him this way and that but almost immediately he found himself back at his table in the middle of writing a letter which he must no doubt have just started writing at the moment the thief was thieving and he continued this letter more or less exactly as if the theft wasn't of this world and then when he'd finished it the Earth for no apparent reason stopped revolving even though he had gone to bed got up and eaten many times and seen a car accident two men fighting a despairing lover trying to understand but finally without any more reason than usual the Earth suddenly decided to become a top once again and fortunately still in the same direction and it did this on the evening when Grabinoulor met a parliamentary candidate's wife in the métro and she gave him a gift voucher taken from a counterfoil book and it gave you the choice between half a pound of chocolate 25 kilos of anthracite 3 packets of tobacco or the honour of stroking the fur of her young angora pussy three times if he would promise to vote for her husband Grabinoulor who is a gourmand who feels the cold who is a smoker et cætera took the gift voucher and congratulated himself on being an elector but no sooner had he left the devoted wife of the trainee-deputy than he found himself all tangled up in an inextricable indecision what should he choose the chocolate the anthracite the tobacco or the angora pussy and this meant that he could no longer carry on in his normal way he practically threw himself on people's noses he trod on toes that were not his own I do beg your pardon Monsieur I'm thinking about the anthracite and the angora pussy not everyone thought this a very sufficient reason and a man in overalls asked him whether he thought he was entitled to tread on people's toes merely because he was wearing a jacket and his fist was on its way to bash in the face of this good-for-nothing who found it amusing to take the piss out of honest working men naturally Grabinoulor disappeared before the blow could strike home but after that he gave the gift voucher to this man of action and went off to walk along solitary paths in the hope of meeting neither woman nor man for a very long time and after he had been walking indefinitely he found himself precisely at dawn in a clearing where a lot of soldiers were drawn up in a rectangle but the sole occupant of one of the shorter sides of this geometrical figure was a man who had been carried there in a state of collapse on a chair nevertheless he and his chair were tied to a stake driven into the ground and he had a very tight blindfold over his eyes and the soldiers facing him raised their rifles took aim and fired and immediately a red patch spread over the man's waistcoat they untied the sitting corpse they took it off its chair they laid it down on the ground and in the morning twilight all the soldiers paraded in front of this man they had killed but Grabinoulor didn't consider all this very admirable and he thought it would be better to abolish the past quarter of an hour so he abolished it and that's why he arrived a quarter of an hour early on the planet where he had arranged to meet himself

## FIFTEENTH CHAPTER

*Grabinoulor uses his nose and pushes himself off on the swing*

BUT YOU CAN'T GO AND LIVE on another planet for very long when you are a man and Grabinoulor's feet liked the earth and the asphalt for he was born on the Earth so whenever he was elsewhere he felt obliged to come back here and sometimes he found himself standing at the foot of a tree in blossom sometimes in the métro where hands with dirty fingernails made his own recoil along the rail and his hands which he liked were not content to recoil but in spite of the friendly glove were seized with a desire to flee very far away from all the dirty fingernails of all the fat fingers that flattened themselves everywhere but on one occasion however he felt like leaving his hand there touching the dirty fingernails so as to be connected through the contact of the flesh to the work of the world and his light hand was very unhappy and the rest of him was not transported as he had hoped by a lyrical admiration for the men of raw material and he merely perceived that they were dirty and that they smelt and he thought architects don't smell as much as building workers do and thus Grabinoulor had an inkling that you could base the classification of society on smells starting from the spirit which it seems has none but this of course only if you assume that the no is preferable to the yes which is arguable and after discussion it might well happen that you reached the point of ending with the spirit instead of beginning with it and he was instantly seized by a great desire to smell men in order to classify them going from the smell-less to the over-smelly or from the over-smelly to the smell-less so he shook himself like a dog coming out of the water and went and sat down in a salon where a very respectable gentleman was talking to two no less respectable ladies or to dot one's i's and cross ones t's where Monsieur Conilatan was saying to Madame Conilatan and Mademoiselle Conilatan well I agree that I don't understand the first thing about all those pictures with neither head nor tail that some of your modern artists paint these days but I've just bought a few real horrors because Dupont who is an erudite man has assured me that throughout the ages there have always been three categories of men the masses who don't understand anything the middling folk who understand some things and the élite who under-stand everything that's incomprehensible and I'm beginning to see these horrors transforming themselves into works of genius now at this moment Grabinoulor stuck his nose out and noted that Monsieur Conilatan smelt of best quality eau de Cologne then as he was already tired of sniffing at people he slid on to an extraordinary swing whose ropes were so long that you couldn't see the heights they were hooked on to and Grabinoulor didn't sit on the seat of what might be called this absolute swing but stood up on it and bending his knees he soon gathered momentum and the oscillation soon reached such amplitude that Grabinoulor disappeared sometimes into the before and sometimes into the after and you could barely see him when he passed through the now and this oscillation was most majestic and impressive to the silently-watching crowd each member of which both desired and feared to mount this extraordinary swing for many of them had been there before simply to sit down and jiggle about a bit draggling their feet on the ground but to go flying up and down like that fellow must be very amusing though very dangerous as for Grabinoulor it was quite obvious that he was greatly enjoying this game because he went on bending and stretching his knees for a very long time to keep up his momentum and what he saw no one would be able to say today for when Grabinoulor finally put his feet on the ground his head was spinning a bit and all he said was that he had encountered the perfumed moment of the previous year when he had been on the road to Menton and eaten the amorous oranges of Sicily whose flowers had known the pomegranate tree and also that he had seen in a bookshop window a copy of the poem he was going to write the following year and also that he had

seen a fifteenth-century painter spending several years real years working
on the picture he was painting and he had painted this picture with so
much adoration that it is still completely illuminating today and also that
he had travelled as far as the day when men will make matter move and
re-form it merely by the radiation of their willpower and among other
things he had seen stevedores unloading ashlars there were two there were
three men lying on the wharf holding hands they shouted Heave-ho and
the lump of stone was lifted just as today it would be lifted by the claws
of a crane and without the slightest chip it went and put itself down on
the ground and when the stone was too big and was difficult to lift they
called an extra man who came and lay down beside the others and
Grabinoulor had thought highly of this perfected levitation for he had
observed that these workers had clean fingernails with half-moons just as a
perfumed body does but unfortunately the swing came down again so he
had no time for any further appreciation of the fortunate physical moral
economic and social consequences of this state of the times to come and
when someone asked him why he had stopped the magic swing he replied
that he had caught sight of himself at the age of 75 and he had thought
himself so ugly and so disagreeable that he had preferred not to risk
seeing himself again too soon but it was all for the best because
Grabinoulor is a man who can't stay put


## SIXTEENTH CHAPTER

*Adieu Adieu trrrrrraou dé kiou* *

ON A SHUT-IN NOVEMBER EVENING Grabinoulor's feet were
sploshing about in the Paris mud and that evening he distressed his shoes
no end they were quite astonished at having to plough through such black
mud when such white snow was falling for Grabinoulor's shoes are full of
logic even when his feet are inside them nevertheless although he was
perfectly conscious—which is something that happens even to people who
are not in the least conscientious—of how humiliating this state was for his
shoes and indirectly for himself too he couldn't do anything that evening
other than place his feet on the ground as there was so little space between
the earth and the sky and that was why even though he was Grabinoulor it

took him a long time to reach the theatre which high-flown declamators were supposed to transport with all its listeners to the environs of the infinite but a gentleman with a nose a mouth round cheeks spectacles ears and a fine mirror-like pate simply by speaking brought the ceiling down on to the head of everybody sitting in the theatre and it was Grabinoulor who was the most inconvenienced by this nevertheless ladies and gentlemen in full possession of their senses—although being in possession of one's senses doesn't always mean that one is sensible—came on ostensibly to make some allegedly poetic revelations but the smart suits of the men-readers remained smart suits and the pretty little dresses of the women-readers remained pretty little dresses during and after just as before and the carved Cupids—for the tenderest representation of love may be carved in the hardest stone—on the stage boxes didn't change places and the colour of the seats remained the same whereas everyone knows that when seats are really deeply affected they change colour and when the audience left it the theatre was still in the same boulevard where white snow that made black mud was still falling which was why they were talking animatedly of the price of butter and the increase in rail fares as for Grabinoulor he opened his umbrella yes really you must imagine as best you can Grabinoulor under an umbrella the fact remains though that they—the umbrella and Grabi—found themselves no one knows either where or when confronted by public opinion whose belief was that the end of the world was nigh not on account of the unfortunate slight planetary impingements predicted for the following Wednesday at five fifteen pm but because of the feminine fashion that was guilty of relying too openly on the beauty of the human body well Grabinoulor realized in time that public opinion is nothing but a hideous toothless old woman that people are in the habit of passing off for an irresistible beauty and he recognized that the world was in perfect and reassuring health since it was virgins who were asked by fashion to reveal the breasts which they have and not grandmothers who only have the remains of them and that was why full of confidence in the future he didn't stay any longer that day than any other day with the old woman with three stumps of teeth and he passed by he walked turned disappeared reappeared and took the train (unless it was the train that took him) now while he was travelling incognito on a suburban line in a bottom class carriage it so happened that at one station a market woman who was truly formidable both because of the fiery colour of her face and the height and width and thickness of her meat got in and settled down

57

comfortably and forever you might have thought in Grabinoulor's compartment opposite a narrow little old woman and Grabinoulor claimed that
from that moment on the compartment was completely transformed
although he couldn't say precisely what had changed then when the train
was just about to move off they saw this mass with its pyrogenetic head
lean out of the window and shout in a resounding and meridionally-
accented voice Adieu trrrrrraou dé kiou then the entire mass came back
and flattened itself on the seat or rather flattened the seat laughing a
magnificent belly laugh but it quickly became serious and addressing the
little old woman said at least you didn't understand what I said just now
oh I'm glad you didn't understand it wasn't very polite you know Madame
what I said just now but I well you know I'm someone who just can't
help making jokes and even though the train had started she leant out of
the window again and fired off her joyous cry at the people in the fields
'Oy you lot Adieu trrrrrraou dé kiou' and that day the train took much
less time getting to Paris even though according to the mechanical
assurance of the clocks in the stations it wasn't running any faster so in
the evening of that day Grabinoulor found himself cooped up somewhere
or other with five or six poets which is as dangerous as watching an
experiment in a laboratory of pyrotechnics because the poet is a species of
mankind who projects coloured lights of a very beautiful effect when he is
on his own but who has the strange characteristic of sending out nothing
but asphyxiating or explosive waves the moment he is in the presence of
another individual of the same species and when six of them find themselves nose to nose the atmosphere immediately becomes unbreathable or
full of sparks which is why it might perhaps be reasonable in order to
preserve oneself if not from the explosion at least from the asphyxia to
wear a boar's-head mask during these gaseous meetings but Grabinoulor is
a being who is both violent and free and who has a horror of anything that
restricts and disfigures him and if he reluctantly agrees to hide his flawless
body under some costume that is both a great liar and full of sadness
exactly as if he were ashamed of this beloved body at least he has so far
stubbornly refused to put any sort of mask over his face Adieu adieu
trrrrrraou dé kiou which is why that evening he felt some slight seasickness
which might also be called salonsickness but when he was back on the
friendly asphalt he breathed in the fresh air deep down into his thorax
Adieu adieu trrrrrraou dé kiou and even though this joyous refrain
produced the sound of a fairground orchestra within the immensity of

himself he could still hear the last breath of a fine painter* who had just died far too soon after his birth in one of those big houses in the City built especially to go and die in and he could also hear the sound made not so long before by the fragile girl with the long pigtails when her little body with the big child-carrying belly flattened itself on the cobblestones after the death of the painter had precipitated her from a sixth-floor window and these muffled sounds created a silence in Grabinoulor and he aged a notch but he continued on his way because he could still hear the monumental woman shouting out between two hearty laughs Adieu adieu trrrrrrraou dé kiou

## SEVENTEENTH CHAPTER

*Grabinoulor is a man*

SHE WAS ONLY OLD ENOUGH to be a girl and yet she was a pregnant woman and Grabinoulor looked at that imaginary face and that positive belly saying to himself because he says a lot of things to himself that he doesn't repeat to anyone else what vandal can have broken that beautiful image by mounting it and he said that to himself because he wasn't the one responsible for her pregnancy for he is always scandalized at the de-florations that other men have allowed themselves and the only pure and praiseworthy women are the ones who give themselves to him the ones who give themselves to other men are both degraded and sinners and even as unforgivable as they are incomprehensible since all things considered you have to  wonder how women can make up their minds to put them-selves in men's arms actually how can men and women penetrate each other when they are precisely made to avoid one another it's a bit like those March days when you see the rain and the sun arm in arm not to say amorously entwined really it's turning all the good peaceable natural laws inside out for no good reason so Grabinoulor discovered that he was rather astonished that men don't love men and women women quite simply birds of a feather flock together and as Grabinoulor isn't in the habit of doing nothing he immediately created a very ordocratic State in which only equilibrated loves were permitted and at first a certain serenity azured this state of simple loves and the lovers were a harmonious sight but soon a

59

certain amount of ill intent became apparent and some men became
women and some women tried to become men and finally Grabinoulor
himself no doubt on account of his already fairly old habit of composite
love didn't quite know whether he was the key or the lock and he was one
of the first to realize to his great astonishment that he could really only
see himself in all his beauty with women his opposites and so as not to dis-
obey his law he left his State though no one ever knew which way and he
has never bothered about it since for at that time an extraordinary thing
happened to him which it seems has never happened to anyone but him

So Grabinoulor came back very pensive from the land of simple
love and without knowing how while he was no doubt nonchalantly
pursuing his train of truant thought he came up nose-to-stomach in a town
that will exist in nine hundred and eighty-seven thousand years from now
nose-to-stomach I say against a pregnant man and he was a superb sort of
man such as he had never yet seen that's to say almost twice as tall as
Grabinoulor himself and he could immediately perceive that all the
inhabitants of this town were more or less of that skyscraper height and
that many of them were pregnant and with his first glance and very naturally
—though we don't really know how and by what—Grabinoulor recognized
the true and noble hidden reason of these formidable bellies whereas
anyone else would on the contrary quite naturally have thought that all
these shapes belonged to a race of super-pot-bellied people because as
these individuals were naked Grabinoulor had been able with his above-
mentioned first glance to make a certain observation which tended to
prove that they were men but on reflection he wondered whether this
proof was sufficient for it was so small so small and so totally devoid of
appurtenances and panache that it only represented a quarter of what
Grabinoulor knew he had between his thighs even though these supposed
men were twice as tall as himself and yet their bodies were all sinuous with
muscles so Grabinoulor was a little surprised but one of these tall walkers
judging from the amazing fashion in which this stranger was dressed that he
must be in the presence of an inhabitant of one of the worlds he didn't yet
know placed a big friendly hand on his shoulder and asked him which planet
he had come from the Earth replied Grabinoulor am I not still on it goodness yes it is certainly the Earth here said the giant with the rabbit's scut but
how can you be an inhabitant of our world when you are so small and so
strangely covered truly you are more extraordinary than the Selenites the
Martians and the spring-like Saturnians although they are pretty surprising

at first sight when I saw you coming from a distance I immediately
imagined I don't quite know why that you had come from the moons of
Saturn with which we are in very close correspondence but none of whose
inhabitants has so far come to shake us by the hand travel is so badly
organized that you have to think twice before coming to see your friends
when you live in the provinces but I am most desirous of making your
acquaintance do please come and have supper with me we shall be able to
chat at our leisure and Grabinoulor accepted because there were a lot of
things he wanted to know and when they were in the house Grabinoulor
saw rather a large number of giants similar to his host most of whom were
pregnant and they asked him at once why his body was covered with
various materials and whether he was absolutely determined to remain in
their midst in such a disguise now Grabinoulor who likes himself much
better naked than dressed and who moreover felt somewhat humiliated by
his short stature had a certain satisfaction in seizing the opportunity
offered him to show all those ten-foot men that there was at least one
respect and not the least important in which he was very greatly superior
to them which is why Grabinoulor immediately took off all his clothes
down to the last item of underwear and they all agreed that it was a great
mistake for him to wear any and that he was a very well-made miniature
being but some of them with a more developed sense of the ordinary
harmonious proportions objected that in the very middle of his body he
had a monstrosity or perhaps a disease and these objections drew attention
to Grabinoulor's genital equipment and they stood him up on a table so
that the monstrosity would be at a convenient height for careful
examination and then they all moved their heads closer and took the
dangler in their fingers and weighed the twins to such effect that the
dangler lengthened and swelled to the great astonishment of the curious
who in their efforts to understand this phenomenon one after the other
squeezed it so hard in their hands to stop it swelling that it very soon became enormous and almost vertical and as Grabinoulor shut his eyes and
grabbed hold of the wrist of the hand that was squeezing him one of the
giants received a jet of human liquid slap in the face and the hand holding
the palpitating part became all gluey so all the 'ten-footers' retreated in
terror because they were kind men and they were afraid that because of
their curiosity they had hurt the stranger but Grabinoulor rapidly regained
his perfect composure and apologized to them but they on the contrary
were sedulous in making their own profound apologies to him and after

these delicate politesses the giants experienced a great desire to go and plunge into the sea water where Grabinoulor followed them in delight and it was not until they were back home and seated round the tall dining table so laden with every kind of sustenance that it looked like a market stall hence a table that was naturally extremely gratifying to Grabinoulor that they asked him to explain what had happened but this question somewhat embarrassed Grabinoulor and he really would have preferred to talk about something else but what happened to me he said is what I think would happen in similar circumstances to every normally-constituted male individual to which the 'ten-footers' replied but all of us here are normally and perfectly constituted although no such accident could happen to any of us for the excellent reason that we have not as you can ascertain for yourself de visu a similar infirmity between our legs and so saying several of them stood up and got Grabinoulor to observe that all they had was a very thin very short slightly pointed conduit which they could guarantee to be of perfect invariability in all circumstances but replied Grabinoulor that's precisely what most bothered me when I arrived here because I couldn't help regretting that nature should have deprived people of such fine stature of the most important thing and I must admit that that was why I didn't hesitate to strip naked and let you examine a bit too closely I agree now my virile equipment in order to prove to you that you are hardly right to be proud of your great height and that it would be advisable for you to recognize my undeniable superiority and this last word made the fat bellies laugh a lot for from the height of their serenity they very sincerely pitied this poor little creature afflicted with such an inconvenience then one of them bent down to Grabinoulor and said sympathetically yes but for goodness' sake we don't need such a long pipe with such transformations to pump our bilge and everyone applauded this flawless argument which was surely going to quell the arrogance of the little individual with the gross deformity but Grabinoulor shrugged his shoulders imperceptibly naturally he said if that was all it was for we wouldn't need so much and what you have might do but my dear friend do you use it to do something else said someone and all the others awaited his reply eagerly what d'you mean do I use it to do something else cried Grabinoulor I should say I do I use it to make love and at the same time to create other beings like me sons and daughters because I make love and I make children but we make children too retorted the giants with one voice and Grabinoulor guffawed and said with what with that and this time the 'ten-footers' looked at one another in amazement for they definitely did not understand why the stranger persisted in connecting 'that' with children and there was a short silence during which Grabinoulor felt himself growing in all three dimensions and at that moment he felt bold enough to say leave me for a while with one of your women and in nine months you'll have the weighty bawling proof of what I'm putting forward a woman repeated the giants looking at one another a woman what's that we know neither the word nor the thing but allow me to say one of them retorted to Grabinoulor that you have to go to a lot of trouble and you need a lot of time to make a child and that in a word this fabrication seems to be quite a business for you not at all said Grabinoulor laughing quite simply there need to be two of you what d'you mean two cried the giants two to make a single child and you call that simple thanks very much enjoy yourself what a lot of difficulties here it's much easier everyone makes his children by himself and Grabinoulor was just about to make a witty remark when one of the 'ten-footers' very obviously the oldest began to speak very slowly and immediately a learned ambience descended on them and they all fell silent and turned their heads in the direction of the venerable toothless mouth that was saying in the voice of a guide philosopher and friend today we have the extraordinarily extra-ordinary good fortune to be seeing what we shall never see again for I now know I am sure that the inconceivable being or more precisely the demi-being now before our eyes is what in prehistoric times used to be called a man a man some of them repeated inquiringly yes a man continued the sage that's to say a being who must have been born in the incalculable past when our species was still in the making for we know that after reflection the beings on the Earth came to believe in the division of labour and they divided into two in order for each to have its own speciality so in those days there were what they called the male and what they called the female each was the opposite of the other and throughout their lives these two halves spent their whole time poking one another both literally and metaphorically and in both the good and the bad sense for clearly the one couldn't do anything without the other and to come back to the question we are now considering it was only by coming together most often fortuitously and in an almost superficial fashion by means of that uncouth male equipment that so surprised us earlier on and which penetrated to a depth of a few centimetres inside the female we don't know exactly where that they could engender and our present-day science can almost positively state that this obligation for the two halves to be constantly coupling was the direct or indirect cause of all the innumerable woes that living beings had to suffer in those dim and distant times of the first ages of the Earth and very particularily so it would seem of our species during which times the male was called man and the female woman and now all of them without saying a word were looking at THE MAN THE MALE and they had religiously moved a little farther away from him and then it was Grabinoulor's turn to speak and he said it's true I am a man and all of you who might you be my dear man said the elder gently we are your descendants yes quite so Nature finally became tired of all the complications she had at one moment got herself entangled in through trying to satisfy I don't know what vague desires for simplicity and I can't tell you exactly how our oneness was brought about the intermediary types are missing in our anthropological collections some types are always missing from collections just at the most important passages what a lot of pages have been torn out of the book of Nature nevertheless the fact is that she finally combined the two halves that she had previously had the bizarre idea of dividing what cried Grabinoulor then you are double no replied the old man on the contrary I am single or simple and I don't understand it's perfectly understandable though then you are both male and female not altogether if that were the case then I'd be double whereas as I'm male-female or female-male whichever you prefer I am simple all right we'll grant that said Grabinoulor but what about love then there replied the sage looking stupid I don't know what you're talking about  and what about children retorted Grabinoulor how do you make them very easily every year during a fixed period when we are neither too young nor too old at certain moments we feel a great joy within ourselves and that's all the child is on its way and three months later we give birth and Grabinoulor asked permission to sit down for he didn't know whether he ought to be dumbfounded but he was undeniably a little surprised and a little confused it is indeed very simple Grabinoulor thought out loud Nature has followed her normal course the old 'ten-footer' replied calmly she has almost come back to her point of departure and she will soon have come full circle which might mean that the manifestations of life on earth are approaching their end and this was not at all to Grabinoulor's liking indeed for quite some time now he had been both afraid of being put in a cage by the wise man and extremely desirous of being back amongst his own kind in his Paris where the streets are perfumed with short-skirted women finally Grabinoulor began to feel well and truly homesick just like a simple villager and that was why he cut the conversation short and returned to his own age but in the avenue des Champs-Elysées while he was busy giving his admiration to two beautiful silky legs walking in front of him he suddenly remembered that he hadn't asked those men-women what gender they belonged to to the fourth no doubt he supposed a gender engendered by the fourth dimension and he returned to the silk stockings alas we don't know the colour of that silk and consequently we don't know the colour of those stockings either

## EIGHTEENTH CHAPTER

*Grabinoulor takes his coffee with kings*

AFTER A LAVISH LUNCH Grabinoulor was savouring the agreeable mixture of coffee and cigarette smoke in his mouth and while his senses were thus sunning themselves his ancestors smiled at him so he straightaway went off to visit the kings of History but he immediately saw very clearly that these kings couldn't be his ancestors because each of them was only the king of a kingdom and he felt far more at home with the kings of legend who as a matter of fact are only one and the same king the master of the spirit to whom different peoples have all given a name and a face and Grabinoulor knew very well that they all resembled each other and that he resembled them as swallow resembles swallow and he felt very much at his ease in their palace from which he could see the poor people of the workaday sort hurrying along the Parisian boulevard going about their business and then he called the waiter and paid and walked off along the pavement quite simply as if he too were a workaday sort of man and some extraordinary things happened to him but the people were in too much of a hurry they didn't notice any of these things and that's why the evening papers said absolutely nothing about them

## NINETEENTH CHAPTER

*A lobster mayonnaise starts the world going again*

THERE ARE SOME DAYS when Grabinoulor's place on the Earth is like that of a flowerless jug on a mantelpiece and when Father Time or the tank whose heart he has practically managed to soften seems to stop counting in spite of the people who are being born and the ones who are dying and the ones who are laughing and the ones who are crying and the ones who are loving and in spite of the mornings and the evenings and anyway Grabinoulor doesn't take undue advantage of this benevolence and he starts the world going again even before the Old Man begins to feel any regrets and therefore everyone thinks that there has been as there is every day a discussion in Parliament a ministerial blunder a new tax a strike a Socialist Congress a new literary review a great boxing match some horse races a brawl a railway accident a shipwreck a serial story and a murder and when Grabinoulor saw that particular lobster mayonnaise lying on its lettuce in the middle of a dish on the table he reckoned that red and green even though complementary colours have undeniable appetizing virtues and various stomachs formed a circle all around this culinary sumptuosity and what had to happen happened after which the world had an exquisite taste and became a masterpiece

## TWENTIETH CHAPTER

*Gee-up Fanny*

THAT DAY Grabinoulor was travelling in a little country which you couldn't see from Paris but which nevertheless existed the moment you got there and Grabinoulor is always amazed when he arrives in a town because this town was only a black dot on a green or pink piece of paper yet when he arrives it's a jumble of streets with their passers-by which he can walk in and houses with their inhabitants which he can go into and he is astonished at the power men have of enclosing in a dot a simple pen-prick streets passers-by houses palaces factories mountains sorrows joys colours noises shapes space and everything that doesn't exist and in that way put on a little square of paper not only little countries like Belgium or Portugal but also the whole of Europe with its immense Russia and the whole of immense Asia with its India and its China and the whole of Africa with its deserts and the whole of immeasurable America and all these lands with their towns and not just tiny little sub-prefectures but capitals containing millions of souls like Paris London and New York and also all the rivers that flow through these lands the most smooth-running as well as the most torrential the most endless as easily as the insignificant little branches and the Atlantic Ocean and the Pacific Ocean and the Indian Ocean with all their islands and probably all their fish and all their waves and all their storms and the Sky which is even bigger they put that on a little sheet of paper too with all its planets all its suns and all its light-years and it was in this little country that they showed him the old shepherdess who had just inherited ten million from her master and the old shepherd who had just married the shepherdess and the old shep-herdess was just passing by she was heavy on the back seat of her old victoria while the old shepherd was well rounded on the front seat driving the old white mare long-haired Fanny and Grabinoulor thought that this too was contained in the little black dot on the map come on gee-up Fanny and it was just at this moment that it seemed to Grabinoulor that Monsieur Herakles had shown very bad taste on his travels just when the road forked even so on second or third thoughts this didn't surprise him because you couldn't expect much better from a man who was so unsqueamish but all this happened the day before and it was now the day after so Grabinoulor had no alternative but to observe that he was late and with a single bound he leapt into his today as he would into a moving train there were some women who were talking so much that he got en-tangled in their conversation and several times went and dropped down into these women's kitchens or their daughters-in-law's bedrooms or their husbands' workshops however seeing that there were two pink cheeks and two blue eyes and a little red mouth opposite him he managed to extricate himself and go for a walk in the sort of spring-like landscape that he preferred and from there he was able to escape and return to Paris

TWENTY-FIRST CHAPTER

*Grabinoulor sells his wardrobe*

I'd like to know what that piece of furniture thinks of me
I often think I'm alone in front of it
Cupboard who are you
Cupboard when will you speak
And to think that there are some people
Who say that you are a wardrobe
And the wardrobe spoke
But after all I'm not asking you for anything
You've lived with other people
You're a whore
And I shall sell you

Grabinoulor is cantankerous so when his wardrobe one day started mumbling something about Pierre or Paul or whoever he decided that it had an unbearable smell so he turned his back on it and an hour later he sold it to someone who said to himself it's a very beautiful wardrobe and when the trollop was no longer in his room Grabinoulor unshook himself washed himself and was rejuvenated but then all of a sudden his other furniture began telling him stories about the people it had known and the very walls started harping on the same theme and Grabinoulor couldn't bear to hear any more and without giving them another glance he got rid of all the aged pieces of furniture encircling him for he was now no longer unaware of the fact that they had all ganged up with the walls to suck his youth out of him while all the time giving the impression of being of some use to him and he went out of the house and the other houses in the streets tugged him towards them each one wanting to talk to him about former times but he passed by all the same and he went on walking until he came to a place where there was no town so he had one built along a very straight line and it was a nice white one which only people of a white age could live or sleep in and into the house that had just been built for him he carried some furniture that had just been made for him

in a form that had just been invented and when he went into that town
and into his house Grabinoulor became a man who had never yet been
used for anything but at that instant both the town and the furniture in
the house must have aged a little because otherwise where would the time
have gone nevertheless the aging didn't show and everything seemed truly
new in that town to which no one has ever given a name for fear of giving
it an age and that's where he's going to live until the next chapter

## TWENTY-SECOND CHAPTER

### The benefits of filth

GRABINOULOR RAISED HIS HEAD and found himself face to face with
a man dressed in a most elegant lounge suit but the authentic filth with
which his hands his neck his face and his et cætera were covered was in
startling contrast to the impeccability of the English cut of his suit and the
whiteness of his collar and Grabinoulor was more affected by the filth
than by the cut and the collar and that's why as lightly as a dancer he side-
stepped at a right angle and the dirty man smiled and held his hand out
very straight for the cordial shake but Grabinoulor's eyes were very busy
in the distance and he looked as if he hadn't noticed it and the dirty man
said in a resounding and laughing voice what you too Grabinoulor you too
refuse to shake my hand which you no doubt don't consider clean but
Monsieur replied Grabinoulor still keeping his distance I don't know you I
rather thought as much replied the man and that's why I decided to cross
your path because it is indispensable for you to make my acquaintance
and I must ask you not to dispense with it for let me tell you that I am an
authenticated descendant of Antæus now as you know my ancestor was
a great deal stronger not only than all the men but even than all the demi-
gods of his time thanks to his mother Terra the Earth who while
pretending not to know him provided him with all the energy-current he
could possibly want and Hercules who was the champion in those days
would never have felled him if he hadn't employed the ruse of cutting off
his current and that gave me a great deal to think about because if we are
at the mercy of a belt then the power that the Earth is fully prepared to
communicate to us won't do us much good and I hadn't found a practical

69

solution until people began to talk about Hertzian waves when I immediately thought that something analogous must happen with the energy of
the Earth which we stupidly allow to go to waste and I say we because I
am quite certain that there is a tremendous chronological error with regard
to Antæus whose date of birth according to my laborious research should
be placed not in the Hellenic period but quite simply in the morning of the
first day of humanity which amounts to saying that we are all the sons not
of that spineless Adam but of the weighty Antæus whom we might as well
go on calling Adam if we don't want to put ourselves to the trouble of
rewriting Genesis and so I told myself that there must be a way of
remaining in constant contact with the earth even when we aren't touching
it and one morning in my bath I became clearly conscious of the state of
insulation we foolishly so enjoy putting ourselves in when we take such
pains to wash our body from top to bottom which body thus relieved or
rather deprived of the protective and conducting particles of the maternal
clay goes its own way abandoned to its own power that's to say to its
weakness whereas on the contrary when it is very copiously covered all
over with a nice layer of respectfully-preserved filth it is constantly in
direct communication with the generative Earth whose honest filth which
it finds attractive picks up all the power-currents meeting all around and
then you have the happiest possible human body moving around omni-
potently in an eternal bath of energy-security in the present and in the
future and ever since that morning I have taken good care not to wash
myself well now in the last ten years I haven't encountered a single man
who even dared to touch me do you understand now my dear Grabinoulor
why I was so keen to cross your path the reason is that genuinely liking
you so much and knowing that you are in every respect worthy of it I
wanted to confide my secret to you so that you too can be invincible
like me a thousand thanks Monsieur replied Grabinoulor I believe you're
right it is a very simple way of getting oneself respected here below and
as always it only needed someone to think of it you deserve the highest
praise but personally I have another way of tapping the courage that
comes out of the earth and I find it more agreeable for in fact each of my
hairs is an antenna and so by courtesy of this bushy mane I am abundantly
provided with nervous juices and I am therefore much more reliably invincible than our father Antæus and just as reliably invincible as you
nevertheless when I meet Delilah or when I become bald I shall remember
your good advice and then and then he passed his hand through his hair

and the man of ancient filth had disappeared and even taken his smell with him so Grabinoulor was free to breathe and he went off in every direction and in the first direction inside a windowless little room in funereal silence and appropriately gloomily lit by the reflected light of an invisible lamp he saw some people huddled together round a golden head that had been carved in stone by a man from the Egyptian Old Kingdom and all their eyes were taking in what remained of its shape and of its gold and the head which was probably quite comfortable in its velvet casing offered no resistance and the dealer was somewhat excited at the thought that he was going to sell it and in the second direction he took his seat in the dress circle of a theatre whence he sank his gaze into the heads geometrically lined up beneath him but he didn't continue this exercise in clandestine penetration for very long because inside those boxes that were either so highly polished by nature or so highly ornamented by hair-dressers and modistes there were so many complications that he was afraid he wouldn't be able to withdraw his gaze without mishap if he sank it into them too often or too far and then in the third direction he saw a man on his way to take some flowers to his wife's grave before he blew his brains out but as a girl happened to be passing he gave the flowers to her instead and they both came back into life but it seems that someone who was with Grabinoulor was extremely surprised and saddened by this and in the fourth direction he was god so as to make revelations of the greatest and weightiest importance to men but he thought it would be better not to waste his time and he went home to get on with the things he had to do and when he got there he found a friend a great English lady who was saying*
jè souis très en colère jè nè veux plus chez moa à Pariss les domstic mâles croyez-vô j'avais une valett què jè pèyè cent quate-vingts francs pèr mois et en plouss jè loui donnè lè couchement lè comm' vous dites cạ lè nourrisse-ment et lè lavement c'était vrraiment raisonnèbeul croyez-vô et bien il m'a fait cett valett grossesses sur grosssssessssses c'est dégoûtant my dear

## TWENTY-THIRD CHAPTER

### Equilibrium

SOME FOLK think that equilibrists are people who are animated by the

71

most perfect spirit of opposition and always ready to challenge the laws of
gravity but others on the contrary think that they are simply the most
obliging servants of the said laws and that their spirit is the most moderate
and the most central that it is possible to conceive of and then again others
think that they are the most perfect type of the good republican because
they have the grearest love of equality and they approach it as closely as is
humanly possible Grabinoulor for his part thinks that equilibrists are
dangerous people because they have offered a high idea of perfection to
men's minds but however that may be he one day had a chance to see the
most extraordinary equilibrists anyone could possibly see and this was not
according to the opinion of the equilibrists themselves but according to
the trustworthy and considered opinion of Grabinoulor and what's more
you too reader will think the same when you hear that this troupe is composed of two chubby three year-old children and an African hound and
the children are almost as tall as the hound but it's impossible to tell
whether they are girls or boys or one boy and one girl and there is no
irrefutable proof that the hound isn't a bitch but apparently that isn't of
the slightest importance for equilibrium well then the hound is sitting very
stiffly in the middle of a little tuft of foliage its body facing the front and
its head facing the side an Egyptian cliché in short and two beautiful
branches that's to say one on either side of the hound diverge gracefully
and subdivide into two nicely-coiled spirals the second one ending in a
flower that rises vertically into the air and each of the children is perched
on each of these lateral flowers well now as there is only room there for
the tiniest tip of one toe each child has one slightly-bent leg elegantly
poised behind him in mid-air like a ballerina and above their heads in their
two upstretched arms they are carrying without even raising their eyes up
to what they are carrying a sort of cup with a very tall stem and the
ensemble of this cup makes a whole that is much bigger than the child
carrying it and on either side of the cup hangs a string of pearls and from
its centre a plant with very tall foliage rises into the air and above it two
intertwined laurel wreaths look as if they're floating as their support is so
light and above them and genuinely looking as if they are not touching the
two wreaths there are two bows whose strings are untied on one side and
these bows are standing on end and they cross one another at an acute
angle and then starting from the intersection of the bows which are at
least as tall as the children themselves is a very delicate helix which shoots
up like the tendril of a vine and supports two little leaves of an unknown

72

plant and above them these leaves are carrying two more intertwined laurel wreaths identical to the ones below and on these two new wreaths a plant with tall foliage is placed upside down in other words this plant is supporting the extraordinarily elongated vase which in reality it is growing out of and above this upside-down plant the very tall vase rises up and then above this vase a branch of roses and finally from each of these immense and so fragile columns supported by each child a luxuriant double-helix bough which is interwoven with the branch of roses goes off at a right angle and the two branches come up as if to form the top of this strange portico and they join each other and are held in place simply by intersecting within a hoop and then garlands of roses are attached to the helices formed by the two branches then at the bottom of the two branches that are linked in the hoop is a little cord from which hangs a huge wreath of roses in which two turtle-doves are loving each other with very tender love* and underneath at the bottom to counterbalance the wreath and the turtle-doves the hound is carrying on the very tip of its head a sort of little tray with a very rounded base on which two crossed keys stand upright and the portico thus formed is a good eight times as tall as the child equilibrists who are carrying it even though they are only standing on one toe lightly poised on the outermost edge of a petal and although Grabinoulor is rather refractory when it comes to enthusiasm he couldn't help at least looking at all this in some admiration all the more so as this state of extraordinary equilibrium had lasted for something like a hundred and fifty years because it was when he was visiting a castle in the purest Louis XVI style that he was lucky enough to enjoy and to take a posed photo of this agreeable folly and on his way back he told himself that the artists of today are very reasonable people but it is no less true that the little old man who was so white so lined so bent was urgently requesting the jostling crowd to arrange things so that his wrinkled hand could apparently accidentally brush against a girl's bosom whereupon Grabinoulor even though he can't be Mephistopheles wanted to give this protracted lover his youth back but the old gourmand had disappeared and the girl went on her way unconsciously taking her little bosom with her

## TWENTY-FOURTH CHAPTER

*Grabinoulor wants to do something stupid* *

ONE MAGNIFIED SPRING EVENING Grabinoulor was all straggly
and he was walking nowhere in particular and for an instant he became
one of those majestic automobiles that are as true as a Greek temple but
he soon stopped being that thing in order to become the perfumed being
made of white skin of black silk of rhythm and of the unknown who
stepped out of it and then when that woman went into a house and therefore stopped existing Grabinoulor walked a few steps farther with her and
not being that any more but not yet being anything else he stopped in
front of a Chinese god who through an immense arched window which was
as perfect to the senses as a mathematical solution is to the mind was
interminably looking at the Parisian Champs-Elysées however Grabinoulor
is incapable of staying in one place for very long even in front of a god
who is both golden and Chinese and so Voluptuousness passed her hands
through his hair for he was at the barber's because that charming lady is
always changing her image and can perfectly well turn into a barber or
even a barber's assistant now as he had forgotten his watch the assistant
obligingly gave him the time and even though he was Grabinoulor he
became something like an allegory with this gift in his hands but he didn't
know what to do with it and he was wandering about like that in a depart-
ment store in great perplexity when the assistant he had asked replied
take the stairs Monsieur really this was too much of an encumbrance for
a man who hates carrying parcels so he dispersed himself leaving both the
time and the stairs behind and he didn't recover himself until the day he
found himself laughing at the story a barrister was telling him about the
liberating judgement that finally made absolute the divorce between a man
and his wife who had been dead for more than a year and it was more or
less at that time on an afternoon with a sentimental sky that a sudden
desire to be famous amongst men was born in Grabinoulor's mind so he
lost no time in opening an inquiry and to this end he had a poster
placarded all over the walls of Paris which said I want to become famous
within forty-eight hours what in your opinion is the stupidest thing one

can do to achieve this result and he added as a postscript in so far as it is
possible I would prefer neither to challenge a black boxer nor to draft a
literary manifesto and that very evening people were talking about it in
Panama a dazzling future was in store for the signatory of that poster
everyone was fully prepared to take him for the genius of modern times
but as the sky had become pagan again Grabinoulor stopped wanting to be
a man of genius so turning on his heel he left his glory in a corner like an
old umbrella and he studied the Tunicata that swim in the sea at Nice and
in the course of this study he learnt that the Salpa enjoy a double and
alternating method of propagation by means of which two different
forms are produced the one isolated and asexual the other aggregated and
sexual which is already not at all bad for inferior animals


## TWENTY-FIFTH CHAPTER

*Grabinoulor meets a sculptor of memories and an etymologist*

ALTHOUGH HE WAS SITTING languidly by some green trees all singing
with birds and breeze one fine morning Grabinoulor thought that life
consists of solid matter in which the living are confined just as closely as a
fossil in its stratum although this doesn't stop men going from Paris to
Rome given that it's the machine that makes the journey and not them
between their morning chocolate and their midday spaghetti but
Grabinoulor didn't consider that to be sufficient reason for him to admit
their liberty nor was this sufficient reason to stop them going about their
business just as if Grabinoulor thought exactly the opposite and for his
part that's what he always does and that's why he cordially welcomed just
as he would have done previously an individual who looked just like
everybody else and who came up to him greeting him too politely and said
Monsieur would you like me to rejuvenate you a little in a low voice just
like a thief who comes up to you in friendly fashion to offer you something on the cheap Monsieur would you like to buy a superb watch it's a
real bargain yes but the offer was very attractive so Grabinoulor tagged
along unostentatiously like a curé following a girl you'll see what a gentle
hand I have Darling so they got to the Rejuvenarium which when
Grabinoulor visited it was in reality a veritable town containing countless

districts and the polite man acted as Grabinoulor's guide this is the district of the people who have been rejuvenated by ten years here are the ones who are twenty years younger than their usual age here are the ones who are thirty years younger here are the ones who are forty years younger here fifty years younger here sixty years well now at the first moment Grabinoulor was simply surprised at not having to be surprised because not only had these people who had been rejuvenated by sixty years not become babes at the breast again but all the rejuvenated people in this citadel the youngest of whom appeared to be about forty and they were by far the most numerous had exactly the look and the face of their registry office age and nothing like the look and the face of the age that the rejuvenator announced which was what Grabinoulor told him without any oratorical circumlocutions but the man went on in a soft voice you think Monsieur that I am a specialized masseur and that you have come to a beauty parlour where we are trying to sell face-lifting masks you mustn't think any such thing Monsieur I don't remove wrinkles I don't raise things that drop this is a state in perfect conformity with the laws of gravity which we mustn't defy too long I don't darken hair either all this is not of the slightest importance and please allow me to let you know that I thought you were less of a super-ficialist and yet said Grabinoulor but he didn't go on speaking because they had come to another district and the doctor simply said here are some individuals who have been rejuvenated by a hundred years and they were countless by a hundred years said Grabinoulor let's carry on replied the other these have been rejuvenated by two hundred years these by three hundred these by four hundred and they were beginning to be far less numerous these five hundred and so on from century to century and the district of the people who had been rejuvenated by two thousand five hundred years was still really quite well populated but beyond these BC ones there were only very few individuals wandering about in the different districts until they came to the last one which had only three inhabitants who were the youngest of all but who according to the doctor-guide had only been rejuvenated by 100,000 years and all of them even the latter looked perfectly normal that's to say they looked like everyone we pass in the streets the same faces the same bodies the same clothes but Grabinoulor had a chat with this one and that one at random and he saw very clearly that they were indeed not of the age of their faces but certainly of the age the doctor had said you are free to choose Monsieur said the man I will give you the age you dream of people are far too much concerned with dates of birth which is a most uncouth way of seeing things it would be a little more dignified if we were to consider that a living being is no more than a column of memories but here I am magnifying things out of all proportion in order to present you with an image that will occupy your mind whereas in reality strictly speaking there is no column nor is there even a colonnette and I wouldn't like you to see a column of memories as being a column of a temple oh no just think Monsieur a memory is so slim and it takes up so little space that a thousand years of memories piled up one on top of the other aren't even a millimetre tall and even less in diameter you can see the column from here and the taller it is so to speak the older the man is so all I had to do was find a way to demolish the said column layer by layer to be able to rejuvenate the patient ad libitum so that's all it is Grabinoulor relatively exclaimed really I imagined that things would be more complicated and above all much more mysterious that's all it is dear Monsieur but I must ask you to believe that it needs a very light touch and you must know that I have even managed to as it were sculpt the column that's to say that I remove or I leave memories at different levels and I even remove or leave halves and quarters and eighths of memories and that way I obtain individuals who look as if they are of rare complexity but who are in fact very average sort of people and I assure you that they make a great impression in salons and in every sort of social gathering where people chat and everyone agrees that they are very charming in society and these particular ones are naturally of no age but that's not all said the man who after all was rather astonishing you must realize that once I had achieved such results it wasn't possible for me to have no further desires and after having rejuvenated so many people I quite simply had the imperious idea of aging a few and as you will be able to judge in a moment I succeeded perfectly all I had to do was create some anticipatory memories on the basis of sensations knowledge and conceptions which will be more or less current among men in ten years' twenty years' or a hundred years' time after which all I had to do don't you see was quite simply to place these memories of the future on the column of ordinary memories whereupon I immediately obtained individuals who are ten years twenty years and a hundred years older than their registered age moreover I must say that these are the individuals whom I find it the most amusing to compose for here I am no longer the person who removes which basically is always a humiliating act but the person who adds and Grabinoulor found it a real pleasure to chat with the very old men with the very young faces who lived in that district but he soon found that he was very undecided as he no longer knew whether he was going to ask this surprising man to rejuvenate him or to age him or perhaps even to leave him as he was but at that precise moment as was only to be expected one day or another a great upheaval occurred which caused these intricate reflections to disappear at a stroke and indeed all the inhabitants of all the districts went rushing over to a strange central building where are they going asked Grabinoulor alas replied the doctor they're running to the tower where I keep all their memories and Grabinoulor too ran over to the Tower of Memories and there he saw the whole population in a terrific mêlée throwing themselves on the piles of memories and strewing them all over the place each man trying to recover his own but even though all these memories were packaged and labelled like pharmacists' powders inevitably in all the chaos there were many errors many mix-ups because the people who couldn't find their own grabbed hold of a few memories belonging to other people which naturally only managed to adapt themselves as best they could and a great crowd was already sweeping back towards all four points of the compass but all the people were running and not bothering about which districts they were entering and Grabinoulor turned round to look for his guide but it was a waste of effort the memory-man had no doubt been pulverized but Grabinoulor was less surprised at that than he was to find himself walking idly in a Paris street and as he remembered perfectly that his own district was Montparnasse he turned left to go to the pont des Saints-Pères and in front of Gambetta-the-frockcoat one of the rejuvenated men he had been talking to earlier stopped near him Monsieur said this man in a simple jacket I liked you it seems that people are always saying this to Grabinoulor as a simple Open-Sesame and I would like to make myself agreeable to you would you care to know what language Adam expressed himself in because I'm willing to bet that you don't know what language Adam spoke well Monsieur I do know and I'm going to tell you it was Celtic Celtic exclaimed someone who happened to be passing and who stopped dead how can you say that Monsieur are you still stuck in Celtomania but Monsieur you're a century out of date and Grabinoulor was a little annoyed because he was afraid that the approaching dispute might degenerate into a civil war but the Celtomaniac withdrew saying with much dignity that this interlocutor was an ignorant fellow I can assure you said the latest arrival to Grabinoulor that those remarks were just the maunderings of an idiot I know what I'm talking

about because I'm a philologist-etymologist and not only was Celtic not
the language Adam spoke but French isn't even of Celtic origin ah
Monsieur do you like etymology for instance have you ever thought about
the word 'tête' etymology teaches us that this word actually means
cranium and that 'têt' is only a fragment of an old broken pot what an
image Monsieur gloomy or gay according to taste and you can't imagine
the mistakes made by people who are ignorant of etymology for instance
above the doors of all the dealers in beef veal mutton and lamb you can
read the word BOUCHERIE and you sometimes even see the perfect
example of this kind of thing namely BOUCHERIE HIPPOPHAGIQUE
now personally I think I may safely say that not a single 'boucher' exists
in France today not openly at any rate because the ones that have goat or
'bouc' sell it as goodness knows what kind of lamb and how many people
say be careful 'il est méchant' now we know very well that 'un méchant' is
on the whole no more than a poor blighter who has rotten luck and here's
another curious thing Monsieur why in the XVIIIth century did they call
the vehicle that transports the dead a 'corbillard' whereas in the XVIIth
century that was what they called a wedding vehicle and we all know that
an 'assassin' is only a hashish-eater who belongs to the sect of the
Hashishin and Monsieur another word comes to my lips and I would like
to ask you to believe that I use this image without the slightest
unbecoming thought it is a word that I want to rehabilitate because it is
admirable and people don't appreciate it help me Monsieur if you can the
word 'con' must have the honourable place in the French language it
deserves in actual fact you probably know that this word designates the
vagina well now 'con' which we see esconced and repeated at the top of
so many pages in the dictionary at the letter C is nothing other than the
famous Latin 'cum'—some professors will not agree with me and will say
that it is the translation of the equivalent Latin word but I prefer to
believe that Latin itself went looking for it in 'cum' and don't you think
that this is an example of men's poetic spirit and do you think that these
same men should be allowed to throw such a strong image into the dustbin
and moreover to use it as an insult seems to me to be questionable and I
am tempted to see this as a singularly misplaced sense of superiority in the
male for in fact the 'con' is not always as stupid as men like to make out
and honestly who hasn't had an opportunity to meet some that were full
of initiative and endowed with the greatest presence of mind and furthermore do men think that it is 'con' only at those moments when they are

not using it they really can be accused of showing a certain ingratitude on this point and even of a lack of the logic they so pride themselves on since to them this word designates both what they admire the most and esteem the least ah if I weren't afraid of boring you Monsieur I would tell you a whole lot of other interesting things such as take the word wheelbarrow 'brouette' which for us precisely designates a bizarre little cart with only a single wheel whereas etymologically—just think how nicely this beautiful word lies on the paper and on the lips—whereas etymologically as I was saying it explicitly indicates two wheels birota and you will observe that here in passing we come across the origin of the proper name BIROT which would show that the person who bears it is not only of course a man with two wheels but also a man who like the heavenly bodies is propelled by double rotation that's splendid Grabinoulor finally said and isn't it the name of a French poet who comes somewhere around the XXth century yes indeed replied the etymologist who was also no doubt an epigraphist and here's what I had occasion to decipher on a stone carved in Phœnician letters that I found not far from the place where in that XXth century or thereabouts there was a town built on a plateau which in still more remote times was dominated by the castle of Marguerite the sister of a king

THE POET PIERRE ALBERT-BIROT
WAS CONCEIVED IN ALGERIA
HE WAS BORN HERE
BEHIND THE PALAIS DE JUSTICE
OF FATHERS AND MOTHERS OF THIS REGION
HE WROTE HIS FIRST DICTATIONS
IN THE LYCÉE OF THIS TOWN
HE WROTE HIS FIRST LATIN COMPOSITIONS
ON THE PARAPET
OF THE WEST RAMPART
HE PLAYED HIS FIRST GAMES OF PRISONER'S BASE
ON THE BEAULIEU ESPLANADE
WHERE HE SO OFTEN USED TO RUN
IN THOSE DAYS HE LIVED
IN HIS FATHER'S HOUSE
AT THE FOOT OF THE EAST RAMPART
AND ALSO AND ABOVE ALL
IN THE CASTLE OF CHALONNES
WHICH DECORATES THE HORIZON OF THE SOLAR RAMPART

Thank you said Grabinoulor this poet naturally interests me very much just as everything very old does and I would very much like to know etymology etumos etumos and epigraphy too here we are now at my house would you like to come up but as this etymologist must have been dead for a long time he refused politely and disappeared so Grabinoulor went in alone as usual and he saw that his concierge who that morning had called out a very merry greeting to him with her bowl of coffee in her hand was this evening dead and he raised his hand to his hat and went up to dress for the theatre

## TWENTY-SIXTH CHAPTER

*Grabinoulor has a chat with his childhood friend Eugénie*

WHEN HE HAD squared the circle and observed that noon was about to strike he discovered that he was suffering from a surfeit both of virginity and of liberty so he began to wonder whether he wouldn't buy back his old wardrobe the fact remains that at the eleventh stroke he suddenly had a full-blown desire to live for a few moments in a life which would contain a nicely-polished apartment with a salon dining room bedroom kitchen and WC and where each of these rooms had its very own furniture and special utensils which were not empty and devoid of conversation like virginal furniture and utensils but gravid and very heavy with memories that's to say mother-things that live with people who every day and for ever will go the rounds of these five rooms stopping in each at the same time and for the same length of time for these are the conditions of good health and good writing and that was why Grabinoulor turned up at about a quarter past noon at the house of Eugénie his childhood friend for he too had apparently had a childhood just like everyone else at the same time as a whole lot of other people and this friend Eugénie even though she was beautiful in both age and shape was the widow of a certain Emile and she didn't know what to do with her youth and beauty which only too often went the rounds of the five rooms at the wrong moment and this caused her mother-in-law to suffer from an unusual kind of seasickness which consequently gave her frequent natural opportunities to pull a long face she who had such a perfect sense of proportion and that was why

81

when Grabinoulor arrived Eugénie was in the salon a room no one should ever dream of being in at a quarter past noon while her mother-in-law was waiting for her in the dining room the room for noon and seven o'clock and not only was Eugénie in the salon at a quarter past noon but worse still she was dressing in it a thing that should normally be done in the bedroom at about eight in the morning whereas what most often happened to her was that she ate in that bedroom and at two in the afternoon what's more which is probably why they say that people who make unnecessary difficulties are looking for midday at 2pm and she also withdrew into the bedroom at any hour much more readily than she did into the room where the little brush was kept even though the latter was especially earmarked and all this obviously proved that there was a serious disturbance somewhere inside Eugénie now when Grabinoulor came in Eugénie before putting on her chemise was casting one last loving look at the beautiful Eugénie gazing back at her languorously from somewhere on the other side of the looking glass and hearing the door open she made a move as if to run away but when she saw Grabinoulor she checked this movement and said oh hullo it's you I thought it was someone and he deposited a flying kiss on his friend's forehead and they went and sat down on the sofa where Eugénie put her beautiful plump white arms round her childhood friend's neck saying you don't know you can't know what it's like to be a widow and Grabinoulor thought it over and solely to occupy his fingers which is always a considerable help to thought he caressed the dreamy tips of his childhood friend's rounded breasts and then she stretched out on the sofa with her back flat on Grabinoulor's knees and she arched her whole body so that her belly was a beautiful satiny cushion all ready for a head and there was flesh all over the place and Grabinoulor still had his hands full of it wherever he put them and as he was still thinking his fingers for a change had delicately begun to curl a few short wisps of Eugénie's nicely-cockled black triangle and after some time he said look Eugénie you can't stay vidual any longer and Eugénie said I've lost my appetite and my hair is falling out well then Eugénie you'll have to find a Great Love at once alas my friend what would the family say if I were to dump Emile's memory in the bottom of an old trunk and Grabinoulor's fingers stopped curling what they were uncurling and extended themselves so that his hand found itself nonchalantly and in very friendly fashion containing the whole of Eugénie's little self and he said it would be much better for you to dump Emile's memory in the bottom of an old trunk once and for all rather than have it so often at your finger tips and it was at this moment that Eugénie squeezed her thighs together but it can't have been because she thought she saw Emile's portrait turn its head and she said to Grabinoulor Grabi I'm going to shut my eyes tell me some love stories or else tell me what you do when you have a naked woman on your knees and while he was smiling at the idea of telling her about some splendid games of fornication with all the palpable relief that can only be inserted in the intimacy of confession between childhood friends the ringing of the telephone electrified them Eugénie said Damn but even so went to answer it Hallo who do you want no I don't know Monsieur Einstein but who's speaking ah I see Newton's ghost yes a little and you'd like to have a discussion with the physicist Einstein I see I'm so sorry you are very kind but I can't tell you anything you've got through to France you must have the wrong continent and she put on her peignoir while Grabinoulor said listen Eugénie why don't you telephone Venus and ask her to do you a favour and send you a Great Love at once and he said that because he couldn't wait for life in the five-roomed apartment to be well ordered again and Eugénie turned Emile's portrait round and combing her hair said do you think so oh well so what I'll try hallo hallo I want Heaven please I should like to talk to the goddess Venus is that you goddess please forgive me for daring to disturb you but I've lost my appetite and I still feel like stripping naked I absolutely need a Great Love before the end of the week could you send me one no I'd rather he had dark hair ah fine yes yes preferably of course rather too much than not enough thank you thank you and that was how Eugénie's Great Love arrived the moment she had hung up the receiver and he was really very tall and generously built but even so he had wings like all the ordinary little cupids and as soon as he appeared Grabinoulor was satisfied and made himself invisible so as not to be in their way during this first meeting and the winged man said when he arrived Madame I have been sent by Venus I am your Great Love and Eugénie offered him some China tea and cakes which do you prefer she asked him and he opted for cream puffs and Eugénie in a most expressive manner assured him that where pâtisseries were concerned her greatest delight was to put a chocolate éclair in her mouth and from these first words even though they were in the salon they had just found their bedroom nicknames and with his arms outstretched for their first interlipping Great Love melodied my Cream Puff and Eugénie sighed my Chocolate Eclair but when Chocolate Eclair's lips were

no more than fifteen centimetres away from Cream Puff's lips Eugénie's
uncle arrived with a great clatter and came in just as the tips of Great
Love's little wings were disappearing behind the sofa and as he was a good
uncle he talked to Eugénie at length about Agathe's migraines Agathe
that's Eugénie's aunt and his children's colics his children that's Eugénie's
cousins and as this Eugénie was not at her ease she finally confessed to
her uncle that there was a flea running around in her chemise and she
couldn't wait to be able to look for it and the good uncle said I quite
understand niece you can't keep that flea I'll see you soon and with his
hand on the door knob he turned round and said it's odd it's as if there's a
smell of love here all right niece look for your flea and she went to see him
out whereupon Great Love rushed over to the telephone hallo hallo the
author of the Kama Sutra please hallo hallo is that the author of the Kama
Sutra no Monsieur you have a wrong number this is Potin the grocer's and
Eugénie came back and turned the key very firmly in the lock my Eclair
my Puff and the two mouths were only twelve centimetres away from one
another when someone turned the door knob very violently Eugénie
Eugénie whatever are you doing my Great Love it's my mother-in-law hide
and in the confusion Eugénie's peignoir had come open so her mother-in-
law exclaimed what you haven't got a chemise on that's a fine way to wear
mourning for my son and when she sat down on the sofa she suddenly
slapped her thighs and said my girl it's incredible but there's a smell of love
here and Eugénie Emile's widow straightaway confessed that she did
indeed have a Great Love and hauling her Great Love up by the wings
from where he was crouching behind an armchair she said to her mother-
in-law here he is but Great Love kept his back obstinately turned no doubt
because he hoped his wings would clothe him to some extent this is
disgraceful Madame said Emile's mother decidedly you are a whore I'm
leaving for ever and Great Love was rather upset at causing this trouble in
the house but Eugénie told him I love you let's say no more about it and
I have no hesitation in sacrificing my mother-in-law to you Chocolate
Eclair Cream Puff and their mouths had not even got to fifteen centimetres one from the other when two voices of pretty women called from
the other side of the door which their no doubt small hands were trying
to open and naturally quick hide it's my friends Léontine and Lucienne
and they both exclaimed as they came in goodness are you still in your
peignoir but whatever time do you get up come on quick get dressed we're
going to the Galeries they have some exceptional bargains and the friends

84

were very disappointed when Eugénie told them she couldn't possibly go
out with them because her mother-in-law was waiting for her to go on
some family visits and as they were sitting on the sofa to give Eugénie
alternately and sometimes simultaneously every sort of encouraging good
reason Léontine soon said to Lucienne can't you smell it and Lucienne
replied yes I've been trying for some moments to define it but continued
Léontine my goodness it's as if there's a smell of love and Eugénie said
well that's quite possible I have a Great Love and here he is and she hauled
him up by the tips of his wings but even more obstinately he only faced
them with his back and they both thought him very personable on
condition objected Léontine that the front fulfils the promise of the back
and so saying they both took an involuntary step and an equally
involuntary look in the direction of his front but immediately these ladies
bade a cold adieu to Eugénie because they were respectable women my
Cream Puff my Chocolate Eclair let's say no more about it I would rather
have you than all the respectable women all the Galeries and all the friends
O Puff and there were barely ten centimetres between their two mouths
when her sister-in-law came in like a gale from the high seas well this is a
fine thing Eugénie there's a smell of love all the way out on to the stairs
what will the family say but there may still be time to save your soul I'll
send you my Father Confessor and fleeing with averted eyes she hadn't
even shut the door when the cleaning woman came and said to Eugénie I
must inform you Madame that I shan't be coming to clean any more
there's a smell of love coming all the way into the kitchen there's no way I
can stay in it alas Madame what will the grocer and the butcher and the
dairywoman say and the mother-in-law and the sister-in-law and the uncle
and the women friends came back into the salon en masse and they all
poured out on to Eugénie the reproaches that were sticking in their throats
trying by this means at least to make her blush and the good uncle a bit
after the others came out with my poor Eugénie what will your aunt say
alas uncle she'll have her migraine alas Eugénie and then when at last they
had all really gone Chocolate Eclair began to shiver a little and Puff said
are you angry with me my Great Love no of course I'm not my Puff I'm just
feeling a bit cold because I've had nothing to do for too long and seeing
him sneeze twenty-six times running Eugénie said my goodness you've
caught a cold so she gave him a silver fox fur which he put round his neck
and it was at this moment that Grabinoulor rotated the stone in his ring
because he was rather bored in his invisibility for it isn't at all funny not

to be seen as is well known to a lot of people who to their great regret are naturally invisible but when Chocolate Eclair saw Cream Puff throwing herself on the neck of this smiling gentleman he exclaimed Madame who do you take me for and what are you doing hanging round the neck of a man and Eugénie laughed a lot and said he isn't a man he's my childhood friend and at first the man with the fox fur was more inclined to trust appearances than Eugénie's assertion for Grabinoulor showed every sign of being a man but they provided Great Love with so many sound arguments that his jealousy died and he held out a friendly hand to Grabinoulor who had just been thinking that Eugénie was a very utilizable woman but even so as Eclair and Puff were visibly thinking of something he himself thought no more about it and rerotated the stone in the direction of invisibility which caused Great Love to say that this childhood friend was very tactful my Puff my Eclair and Great Love sends his fur collar flying on to the sofa and Eugénie drops her peignoir which she didn't need and at long last their mouths and their skins were going to touch when the heartless ringing of the telephone came between the two of them hallo who's speaking Emile Emile who but it's me Emile your husband and Great Love had picked up the earpiece yes my Poppet it's me all right they've just installed a telephone to the Earth so naturally my first call is to you my Poppet what a lovely surprise and how are you since I've been dead not too well oh good that's what I was hoping and tell me what kind of mourning you wear for me describe the dress you have on at the moment satin oh satin that's not much like mourning very high-necked I'm glad you told me that because I'm still jealous I have the impression that I can see you you must be very pretty in widow's weeds but it's odd Poppet there's a sort of smell that's reaching me with your voice a smell that reminds me of the Earth it's very odd it's the smell of love and Eugénie put the receiver down and said really it's too much they all think there's a smell of love here but I can't smell anything neither can I said handsome Chocolate Eclair and once again the insistent automatic noise left them speechless and they'd both had their bodyful of it and they looked at each other not laughing he was standing near the phone and she was lying rather heavily on the sofa good god said Great Love hallo who Madame Dubois ah she's my dress-maker said Eugénie lightly going and taking the phone and after that they found themselves back on the sofa where Eugénie said what an idea installing the telephone for them and while she was thinking of all the unpleasantnesses that might ensue she was letting her hands wander at random and as you might say unconsciously trace the outlines of the anatomical treasures of her Great Love who was no doubt a little ticklish because he suddenly grabbed hold of her and put his arms round her waist but even so the authoritarian ringing unlocked his arms and without hesitating this time Great Love leapt up and started a conversation yes indeed you've got the right number and yes your Poppet is here stark naked on the sofa and I'm her Great Love piss off and leave us in peace seeing that you're dead and leaving the phone dangling Chocolate Eclair flung himself on Cream Puff with all the vivacity of a man determined on twofold bliss and Grabinoulor even though he was invisible turned round to the side where there was only the furniture to be seen and yet truth to tell he could easily have had the curiosity to find out whether the wings didn't rather get in the way as for the two mouths on the sofa this time there was no possible doubt that they had arrived at their destination and very shortly afterwards Puff wanting to put a bold front on it was saying my love what are you doing when the clock was hurled down from the mantelpiece followed by its brothers the candlesticks and a chair was chucked from one end of the salon to the other and the display cabinet was pushed over flat on its stomach on to the  parquet floor with the tinkling heart-rending sound of fifty precious pieces of porcelain dying and naturally in spite of the imminence of the gift this had the immediate result of displacing Great Love's ideas and the rest as well so Grabinoulor could clearly see that he wouldn't disturb them quite the opposite if he stopped being transparent and he went and sat down by Eugénie who said to him it's terrifying I'm sure it's Emile and Grabinoulor was obliged to agree that this orgy of destruction which was in such bad taste could indeed only be an energetic and desperate protest on the part of Emile who couldn't resign himself to see even from the heights of the beyond another man so precisely taking his place and Eugénie was now sitting with her legs and arms crossed while Great Love was striding up and down with his hands behind his back and they were all three agreed that this Emile's unreasonable demands were absolutely intolerable but what can we do said Eugénie kill him again Grabinoulor very happily advised her you'll never make love properly until you've got rid of that mean ghost who has nothing else to do he'll always come and sleep with you and lie between your two bellies and Great Love growled that'll be charming and Eugénie said that's quite possible but how do you get rid of a ghost oh said Grabinoulor it's very simple all you have to do is make him explode

explode do you really think so said Eugénie I'm quite sure of it replied Grabinoulor you must invite him to come here and tell him quite clearly that you want to see him with your own eyes and then in order to please you he'll want himself to be more or less opaque and he'll concentrate himself into a point in space and at that moment he'll be explosible and all you'll have to do is strike a match or even better use an automatic cigarette lighter and Great Love took Grabinoulor's hand and pressed it most affectionately saying what an invaluable friend you are but Eugénie was a bit scared because she wasn't used to assassination and the two men lavished the necessary encouragement on her to the accompaniment of tenderly comforting caresses and Grabinoulor was more and more of the opinion that this childhood friend was even so a woman and his hands were now nonchalantly wanting to return to the good places they'd been in earlier which is why Great Love was afraid that Eugénie might catch cold and he was of the opinion that she should put some clothes on and that he should as well because that would be more prudent on account of the explosion and furthermore because it would be a more decorous way to receive Emile so Eugénie went to bury herself in her widow's weeds while Grabinoulor lent his overcoat to Great Love who in order to put it on had to take off his wings which they carefully wrapped in tissue paper and laid out in a drawer of the semi-Louis XV chest of drawers

So following Grabinoulor's good advice everything was blacked out to receive what remained of Emile for as everyone knows ghosts have an unconquerable abhorrence of broad daylight whereas the ghost is on the contrary by his very essence inseparable from absolute light but light within light doesn't delineate anything on our retinas so if the ghost wants to be seen he is obliged to come where it is dark for our pleasure and not at all for his as people seem to think and this is quite definitely an enormous pain that he inflicts on himself in order to satisfy us so we shouldn't be surprised that his visits or rather his visible presences are rare but these considerations interested neither Puff nor Eclair and Eugénie trembling a little asked for her husband to come to the telephone and naturally he lost no time in doing so and in her most intimate voice Poppet persuaded him that she could think of nothing but him and that she had the doubly legitimate desire to see him with her two eyes and maybe even to touch him with her two hands immediately and Emile in a panic promised Poppet that he would come and see her and that he would make himself as handsome as possible so that she could see him even though that would by very dangerous for him for the dead are expressly advised not to show themselves to the living (which incidentally is not very nice of us vis-à-vis the living) but so what said Emile no matter what may happen since you want me I'll come and Eugénie all soft and woolly had only just put the receiver down when Emile appeared because the dead do things so quickly but as instead of a man there was a sort of vaguely luminous bladder hovering in space more or less on a level with her eyes Eugénie tried to cry out and Emile said to her in ghost's voice which even so was humanly articulated here I am Poppet it's not possible replied Poppet you aren't a bit like your portrait go away you scare me alas said Emile this is the best I could do but it really is me all the same it's not possible declared Eugénie go away I can't do anything with a husband who has neither hands nor mouth nor anything oh that's of no importance my dear widow of no importance that's what you say but personally I need to be fondled listen Emile I've had enough and the way you are now are you capable of giving me a child no well then go away and be an angel in heaven and let me make love here what did you say Poppet in that case I'm going to stay more eternally than ever you're going to stay are you well then too bad for you come here my Great Love and Great Love rushed up arms and lips outstretched et cætera when a sort of electrical discharge separated them hurling Great Love on to the floor and Emile-the-Bladder began to whistle with who knows what lips the tune of a sentimental ballad and this ballad was the one they had sung Emile and Eugénie when they were engaged and Eugénie listened to the song and imperceptibly but irresistably edged nearer to Emile which is why Great Love began to wonder whether he wouldn't do better to drop this delayed-action widow whereupon Grabinoulor saw at a glance that he had to precipitate matters in order to save his childhood friend so he grabbed hold of her just at the moment when she had got to a totally unaccept-able distance from the whistling ghost and led her off to the bedroom which had the triple result of in the first place causing Great Love to make a dive for the delighted Eugénie and in the second place of blowing the whistle on the poor inadequate Emile and as an immediate consequence of bringing Eugénie back to her senses or more precisely of bringing Cream Puff back to Chocolate Eclair and as she was now well aware of the danger she had just escaped as well as of the ridiculous situation Emile had just put her in by inveigling her into a whistle to the point where everyone might have thought she preferred the tune of a sentimental ballad to the beautiful reality of Great Love she grabbed hold of the box Grabinoulor was holding out to her and going up to Emile with what they felt was unshakable determination she struck a match and without a word the ghost exploded and this explosion of Eugénie's first husband contrary to all their fears was very calm and caused no damage in the salon but Eugénie was now a little relaxed which is usually what happens to people who have just committed a crime passionnel so Great Love carried her over to the bed in the bedroom which pleased Grabinoulor very much because it proved that order was very naturally beginning to be restored in the house so he himself picked up the clock the candlesticks the chair the display cabinet and the pieces of porcelain and when everything had been carefully put back in place he told himself that it would be good to have some precise information about Emile because you never know how many tricks a ghost may have up his sleeve and he immediately telephoned and someone answered that Emile wasn't there any more because he'd had an accident and he was now a calf that was just being born in a cowshed in Oceania to which Grabinoulor replied thank you very much and I'm sorry to have disturbed you and while he was looking with some satisfaction at the now-orderly salon he remembered that Great Love was in the bedroom with Eugénie and he was suddenly very much afraid that the impatient fellow might have been disorderly enough to take advantage of the situation to begin to make Puff happy so he burst into the room without knocking but luckily Eugénie was so tired that she had dozed off and Great Love not liking to disturb her was watching her sleep which didn't stop her opening her eyes at Grabinoulor's bang-crash-wallop entrance and she opened her arms to him and Grabinoulor solemnly said to them now my friends all is well and you will be able to marry because I certainly hope that you aren't even entertaining for a single moment the idea of sleeping together before that legal ceremony and he requested Great Love to leave the room where the bed was assuring him that Eugénie would become his verso just as soon as the offices of the registrar would permit because if he Grabinoulor were to be able from time to time when he felt like it to come and contemplate or disturb the beautiful order of the life in the five-roomed apartment the first necessity was that Eugénie should be a guaranteed legitimate wife bathing in the esteem of her family her friends her cleaning woman the grocer the butcher the dairywoman only he wondered whether he should or shouldn't tell her that Emile had become a calf but finally an accidental injection of generosity assured him that it would be better not to rob her of her appetite seeing that she was so fond of escalopes and as he had then seen nothing more of any interest in all this he was a long way from Eugénie's house before he realized that he had left it and after he had scattered Eugénie to the winds of the street together with her Great Love her family and her apartment he amused himself by insulating the sphericity of the globe and we don't know for how long a time he amused himself with this human game because he had first of all insulated himself from time


END OF THE FIRST BOOK

Page

19     'While Grabinoulor was under an oak tree an acorn fell on his head . . .'
See *The Fables of La Fontaine*, Book IX, Fable iv: *Le Gland et la citrouille.*

35     'But saintly men / Said hide that breast . . .
See Molière, *Tartuffe*, Act III, Scene ii:
    Couvrez ce sein que je ne saurais voir.
    Par de pareils objets les âmes sont blessées,
    Et cela fait venir de coupables pensées.

46     Gun dogs (bitches) in France were often called Diane.

48     The poem comes from Albert-Birot's *La joie des sept couleurs* (1919).

50     'little Matoum'.
Matoum is the 'true poet' in Pierre Albert-Birot's 1918 play for marionettes, *Matoum et Tévibar.*

51     'the cellaress of the Kingdom of Satan'
See La Fontaine, Book III, Fable vii: *L'Ivrogne et sa femme.*

56     'Adieu adieu trrrrrraou dé kiou'
'trrrrrraou dé kiou' means, literally, 'arsehole'—more or less. Added to the 'Adieu adieu' it forms a popular catch phrase, pronounced in a merry meridional accent, which is not particularily 'vulgar'.

59     Modigliani, who died in the Hôpital de la Charité in Paris in 1920. His companion, Jeanne Hébuterne, pregnant with their second child, committed suicide on the day of his funeral.

71     What the English lady is trying to say is that she is very angry, and will never again employ Parisian menservants. She had one whom she paid a hundred and eighty francs a month plus his board and lodging and laundry, which she considered extremely reasonable,

but he was nevertheless always very very rude to her, which she found disgusting. Only, instead of the proper word for laundry, the lady says 'lavement', which means enema. And instead of saying he was perpetually rude to her, she says that, time after time, he made her pregnant.

73    'two turtle doves are loving each other with very tender love . . .' See La Fontaine, Book IX, Fable ii: *Les Deux pigeons.*

74    The French title of this chapter is 'Grabinoulor voudrait faire une connerie'. For the etymology of the word 'connerie' (from 'con'), see the etymologist's explanation in the twenty-fifth chapter.

## MAKING FRIENDS WITH GRABINOULOR

Poetry is the realm of the divine.
To be a poet is to go beyond yourself and
find the inaccessible in man.

*P. Albert-Birot*[1]

*Grabinoulor*—it's impossible to speak about it. It's a name I found
from its musical sound. I can say that this book came to me one
morning, in the middle of a forest by the sea, in the south west of
France, during the war. There I was, away from everything, and one
morning, just like that . . . the general idea of the book came to me
. . . So far, there must be six volumes written, and pretty substantial volumes at that, as they contain not a single comma or full
stop. They are masses, verbal masses. I work very little on them,
that's to say for one hour every evening, but after forty years, this
adds up to quite a few lines![2]

*The epic,* Grabinoulor, *is the work of a whole lifetime, written con-
currently with the rest of an œuvre that comprises poetry, plays and
novels, all of whose paths frequently cross.*

*Grabinoulor, like every good citizen, has a birth certificate, and I
cannot deny the emotion I felt when I found his family tree in Albert-
Birot's little home-made pocket notebooks. PAB's[3] memory of this vital
event in his life was in no way at fault. He described himself in the pine
forest in Royan, in May 1918, putting the finishing touches to* La Joie des
sept couleurs, *his first great poem sequence.[4] With his pencil pointing up
into the air, he was dreaming of what he was going to start next, when he
had the sudden revelation of THE BOOK. He saw the name of the hero,
the nature of the adventures, the form, and he knew from the start that
Grabinoulor would be his companion for life. The little notebook is
confirmation: Without a break,* Grabinoulor *follows on after* La Joie . . .
*Few erasures, 6 pages dashed off at fever pitch; PAB was so sure of himself
that, under the title, he wrote: (Fragment). And it is this text that
appeared in 'SIC' in June 1918.[5] (See overleaf).*

# Grabinoulor

### (Fragment)

Ce matin là Grabinoulor s'éveilla avec du soleil plein l'âme     il avait le nez droitement au milieu du visage     signe de beau temps     et la couverture étant légère on pouvait d'un seul coup d'œil se convaincre qu'il n'avait pas seulement l'esprit virilement dressé vers la vie
    Cependant qu'il lavait avec joie son corps poilu il fit des bonds tout nu à travers bois et publia un livre puis il mit ses vêtements     il eut même quelques compliments de son implacable amie la glace qui n'a pas coutume d'en faire à la légère     puis immense il s'en fût dans la rue
    deux jeunes filles passaient à bicyclette il vit des jambes et des dentelles et ne sut laquelle choisir ils étaient encore tous les deux occupés à se battre quand les deux désirées allaient disparaître furieux alors de voir que la route allait les prendre celui qui voulait la robe blanche et le chapeau noir porta un coup si décisif que l'autre fut tué et si bien anéanti qu'il fut impossible de le retrouver ni dans ce monde ni dans l'autre     Grabinoulor est plus fort que toutes les machines et surtout les jours où son nez se redresse tel que ce matin là par exemple     puis puis il prit la jeune fille qu'il avait choisie et continua son chemin     presqu'aussitôt il en rencontra une autre qui marchait à pieds et comme elle était seule Grabinoulor n'eut pas d'adversaire il la choisit tout de suite et il allait toujours avec allègresse de plus en plus et quoique les ombres des arbres s'essayassent à lui barrer la route il passa par Paris où il n'eut aucune aventure parce qu'il pensait à autre chose et il revint immédiatement dans la ville qu'il habitait     en passant sur le haut d'une falaise il bâtit une maison admirablement bien comprise pour l'hiver et l'été peinte en jaune et en vert il n'eut pour cela besoin ni d'échelle ni de pots de couleurs ni de pinceaux et tandis qu'il était occupé à construire une machine pour transformer le mouvement de la mer en lumière électrique il s'étala sur le sable et faillit partir pour l'Espagne mais une fourmi l'en empêcha car Grabinoulor est bon et observateur et la fourmi avait beaucoup de peine à gravir la montagne qui sans cesse s'écroulait sous son poids c'est alors qu'il fit un trou avec sa canne pour voir ce que ferait la fourmi mais comme il était très fort il creusa trop profondément et sa canne passa de l'autre côté comme il aimait beaucoup cette canne qui le lui rendait bien il la suivit mais comme la ville dans laquelle il entra était dans la plus grande obscurité et tout endormie et qu'il ne la connaissait pas il eut peur de ne plus retrouver son chemin et peut-être aussi de se faire prendre pour un assassin il revint donc immédiatement de ce côté-ci mais comme le soleil s'était assis à sa place il préféra ne pas le déranger et s'en fut dans l'année prochaine voir si la guerre était finie et quand il rentra chez lui d'un pied léger il dit a sa femme     allons-nous bientôt déjeuner j'ai grand faim

PIERRE ALBERT-BIROT

[*From 'SIC', no. 30, June 1918, original size 225 by 275 mm.*]

*This was PAB's greatest experience of parthogenesis.*[6]

\*

*Albert-Birot warned us: it is impossible to speak about* Grabinoulor. *He was certainly right, and you will be convinced of it by now. The only purpose of this 'postface' is to give you some information, after you have read Barbara Wright's translation of the First Book. I would like to add that this edition gives me twofold pleasure: in the first place, that of following the epic of the hero in a language the only words of which his father knew were; 'Good morning. Please give me some bread.' With this passe-partout, PAB calmly asserted, anyone can go round the world—a remark that would have come well from Grabi's mouth. My second pleasure comes from imagining that a young publishing house necessarily had to be called ATLAS for it to decide, equally calmly, to give our neighbours across the Channel a chance to get to know 'all Grabi'. He has strong shoulders, the young giant who, just as in the* Equilibrium *of the 23rd. chapter, first had the good idea of climbing up on to Barbara Wright's 'main à plume'.*

\*

*Once the first chapter was published, the history of* Grabinoulor *resolutely merges with that of its author. The next 24 chapters followed, and in July 1921, THE FIRST BOOK OF GRABINOULOR COMPOSED BETWEEN 1918 AND 1920 BY PIERRE ALBERT-BIROT appeared, published by Editions 'SIC'.*[7] *The first book, because it was indeed a question of 'Work in Progress'.*[8] *PAB was already making a rendezvous with his future readers. As for the dates, they are strictly accurate. The little notebooks—them again—bear irrefutable witness to this.*

*Almost immediately after the publication of the first book, PAB was at work again, and he added a 26th. chapter, the one about* Eugénie, *Grabinoulor's childhood friend, after which he began to write the second book. From this moment on, he was to devote himself to working in the same way as Montaigne—one of the writers he most admired. The 1921 edition was subjected to erasures, additions, deletions . . . although at this point they were still relatively discreet.*

*In 1933 he at last met the publisher of his dreams, Robert Denoël,* who agreed to publish the first two books of Grabinoulor *in his collection 'Loin des Foules' ('Far from the Crowd')—he was prudent! It was he who suggested that the book should have a subtitle. PAB shuddered at the word 'novel', but was so pleased with the term 'epic' that he forgot whether the idea came from him or the publisher.*

*Two books in one volume, then; twenty-six chapters in the first, thirty-one in the second. And once more everything started again.*

*Albert-Birot filled enormous ledgers with the 3rd., 4th., 5th. and 6th. books, which he reread/revised on successive occasions—always dating them—pen and erasing knife in hand, and in the meantime the Denoël edition became so enriched with paste-ons and so modified that it took long weeks, if not months, of spare-time work to establish the definitive version.[9] [10] Another important modification: Albert-Birot added a heading to each chapter. It is from this 'revised and corrected' text that the translation you have just read has been made.*

*

*A penultimate word about the terrestial adventures of* Grabinoulor. *Albert-Birot's good friend Jean Follain put pressure on Jean Paulhan, of Gallimard, urging him to bring out a new* Grabinoulor. *Follain's obstinacy carried the day, but the book that appeared was a mutilation. It consisted of extracts from the Ist., IInd., and IIIrd. books, which was confusing to new readers, because while there is, of course, no continuity in Grabinoulor's adventures, there are nevertheless various clues, cross-references, hints, that create a whole network of subtle and delectable complicity between author and reader. None of this, however, escaped Barbara Wright at the time. When the TLS sent her the book to review, she wanted to do things properly . . . and found herself in Albert-Birot's library, almost trembling with emotion and barely able to tear herself away from the abundance of documents there.*

*And my last word: a young publishing house, Les Editions de l'Allée has just courageously decided to make Albert-Birot's prose available to the reading public, just as Rougerie has done for his plays and poetry. Les Mémoires d'Adam has just appeared;* Rémy Floche, employé, *is almost in the press, and ALL* Grabinoulor *is looming on the horizon.*

*Good luck to everyone! And from Albert-Birot:*

# Postface

Greetings my reader in a century to come in a thousand years give me your hand and tell me that I'm likeable[11]

*—Arlette Albert-Birot*
*Paris, June 1986.*

1  Cahiers littéraires de la R.T. F. (Radioffusion-télévision française), *2nd. year, no. 3, 3-16 November 1963.*

2  *These previously-unpublished lines are taken from a radio interview given by Albert-Birot to Georges Pitoëff Junior in May 1956.*

3  *PAB was the nickname his friends liked to give Albert-Birot, and with which he signed several of his paintings.*

4  La Joie des sept couleurs, *Paris, Editions 'SIC', 1919,* then in Poésie 1916-1924, *Paris, Gallimard, 1964, and* Poésie 1916-1920, Mortemart, Rougerie, 1986.

5  *From January 1916 until December 1919, Pierre Albert-Birot ran a review, 'SIC', of which there were 54 numbers. It may easily be consulted in the 1973 reprint published in Paris by Editions Jean-Michel Place.*

6  *I say 'greatest', for he experienced several in 'the realm of the divine and the inaccessible'. See Jean Follain,* Pierre Albert-Birot, *Paris, Seghers, 1967, Collection 'Poètes d'aujourd'hui', 'Parthénogénèse', poem, p. 173.*

7  *Atlas Press has based its cover typography on this edition.*

8  *Apropos of Work in Progress, it is as well to bring up the question of Ulysses. In this period of literary effervescence, PAB kept a careful record of the dates. In his Grabinoulor, he noted that the French edition of Joyce's book, published by Shakespeare & Co., appeared in February 1922, and had been preceded by a reading in Adrienne Monnier's bookshop in 1921. This precision, of course, because of Molly Bloom's soliloquy.*

9  *On which PAB also made the odd correction!*

10 *(Additional note by B.W.) Comparing the first version of the first short chapter of* Grabinoulor, *reproduced in facsimile on p. 96, with the definitive version, I have found, at a rough count, at least 27 variations ... (Also apropos of the facsimile, I note that in 1918, for those of his readers so fainthearted as to wonder where the punctuation had gone, PAB gently encouraged them by leaving a few spaces.)*

11 *From 'Siècles', in* Les amusements naturels, *Paris, Denoël, 1945.* then in Poèsies 1945-1967, *Mortemart, Rougerie, 1984, p. 53.*